After a few st heels of her s... down i...

"What's wrong?" Conrad stepped over and steadied her arm.

"I think I'm stuck," Katrina confessed. When he'd taken her arm, she'd realized how tall he was. Of course, she'd shrunk an inch when her heels slid down in the mud.

Conrad frowned. "Hold on to your hat," he said as he scooped her up and settled her into his arms. "There. I'll get you to the asphalt, at least."

"You don't need to—" Katrina started, but he was already walking with her. "Being swept off my feet like this is really quite romantic. You know, like those old movie stars." She was very close to him and it gave her a dizzy feeling in her stomach. His eyes were dancing with laughter.

"If you want movie-star romance, here it is."

And with that, he kissed her.

Books by Janet Tronstad

Love Inspired

Love Inspired Historical

JANET TRONSTAD

would never presume to tell anyone who they should marry. But she does admit to a little matchmaking between the pages of her twenty-some books. She has a series of contemporary and historical books set in Dry Creek, Montana (based loosely on the small Montana town where she grew up). Another four-book series, sharing the lives of four young women in the Sisterhood of the Dropped Stitches, is set in Old Town Pasadena, California, where she currently lives. Janet is a full-time writer and, when she's not at her computer, she enjoys spending time with friends and family.

Wife Wanted in Dry Creek

Janet Tronstad

Steeple
Hill®

Published by Steeple Hill Books™

STEEPLE HILL BOOKS

Steeple
Hill®

Recycling programs
for this product may
not exist in your area.

ISBN-13: 978-0-373-81474-9

WIFE WANTED IN DRY CREEK

www.SteepleHill.com

Printed in U.S.A.

He who finds a wife finds a good thing
and obtains favor from the Lord.
—*Proverbs* 18:22

For my nephew, Orion MacDonald, with love and prayers that, in due time, he will find exactly the right wife. Meanwhile, of course, he's more concerned with his puppy. And getting through the second grade.

Chapter One

Katrina Britton stood looking out the window of the only gas station in Dry Creek, Montana. The handful of houses she saw had their curtains drawn. It was supposed to be spring, but winter still had a grip on this tiny town. The ground was sprinkled with frost and dried mud was splattered on everything from parked cars to that little garden gnome sticking up in someone's dead lawn.

In all her thirty-two years, Katrina had always liked winter. But seeing how lonely the gnome looked surrounded by all that withered grass made her eyes tear up so she blinked and concentrated on the window in front of her. The ground wasn't all that was frozen. Twenty minutes ago, she'd pulled off the I-90 freeway outside this town to take a call on her cell phone. When she finished the conversation, she knew her new photography business was as cold and lifeless as anything she could see out this window. In the past couple of months, she'd fought against everything—her unsupportive boyfriend, her dwindling savings and her own doubts—all in hopes of landing this one big client that would jump-start her career as a freelance photographer. She wanted this more than anything she'd ever wanted. And just when she thought it was hers, the client had said they couldn't use her photos because, although they were technically good, they lacked heart.

Lacked heart? How could they lack heart? She'd spent almost everything she had getting the perfect models to portray that illusive thing called heart.

Not knowing what to do after that call, she started the car again, only to have the muffler make a horrid noise and begin spewing out black smoke. She was forced to take the first exit she could find to get help. So, here she was. Her day was miserable and it was only eight-thirty in the morning.

She hiccupped and saw the man at the

desk look up at her. In an effort to stop the tears from falling, she turned back and focused on the window. Eventually, she'd need to decide what to do next in her life, but for now she just needed to breathe. Of course, a distraction would help her get through the next few minutes, but there was nothing more to see outside. That's when she noticed that the large glass pane itself was amazingly clean.

"Who does the windows?" she turned to ask the man who was watching her instead of tallying up a repair estimate for her muffler.

"I do them," he answered a little tentatively. "Why, do you see a spot?"

She'd grown up in a muddy town like this so she knew how hard it was to keep windows clean during the winter. "I just think that whatever they're paying you to keep them looking like this, it's not enough. You're doing a great job." She peered at his name tag. "Conrad."

She would love to have someone tell her she was doing a good job—at anything. It would certainly make her feelings of failure a lot less right now. But he didn't seem to care if anyone appreciated his efforts. He grunted and turned back to the repair estimate he was filling out.

Well, Mr. Congeniality he was not. She studied him anyway because she needed to focus on something right now. His brown hair was cropped close, but not styled. His beige uniform had his name, Conrad Nelson, embroidered on the top pocket in orange thread. She'd guess he was in his late thirties. He was fit, but not buff. The shirt of his uniform was neatly tucked in and his shoulders were military straight as he sat in his wooden chair.

Something about him steadied her, though. His demeanor said he was a rock. She guessed he was a man who always quietly did his duty.

He pointed to the small sign by the door. "This is my place. I take care of it all. Top to bottom, including windows."

"You're fortunate." She envied him; there'd been pride in his voice.

"I do okay. Moved everything here from Miles City a few months ago." Conrad paused to look at her some more. "You need a job or something? Washing those windows wouldn't pay much, but—"

She tried to smile at him, but couldn't.

"I'm just passing through," she managed to say. When that didn't seem like enough, she added, "This place is wonderful, though."

Actually, the town looked like it had sprung up in some rancher's field and would blow away if a good wind bothered to come along. The only thing that connected it to the outside world was that winding asphalt road she'd driven into town. Across the street from the gas station, she'd seen a hardware store and a little farther down was a café. That was it for businesses, unless she counted the small church.

She wished she could overlook that church, but it stood out. The old-fashioned white building had concrete steps leading up to the front door. Stained glass windows lined the side. If it had a steeple, the place would look almost like the church she'd gone to as a child. That had been so long ago. Back then, she believed God was in His heaven and all was right with the world. Of course, she knew better now. If God was up there looking down at her life, it was only idle curiosity that moved Him.

She blinked. That bothered her more than it had in a long time. And made her feel like she had too much in common with that old garden gnome out there, standing isolated and frozen in some eternal winter she didn't understand. She blinked again. She'd always made do with what she had in life; she would again.

Just then she heard the faint sound of a sliding chair. She turned and saw Conrad reach into a side drawer of his desk, take something out and stand up.

"Here." He opened the box of tissues and held it out to her. He didn't even look at her when he offered the box with the yellow flowers on it. She wondered how often women burst into tears in his office. She hated to look that emotional. Her boy-friend—well, ex-boyfriend now—always walked away from her when she cried. And the tears had come too easily ever since the lump in her breast had turned out to be cancer. The doctor said the surgery had probably removed it all, but he wouldn't know for sure until six months had passed. She had four and a half months left until the final verdict.

"I don't need anything." She lifted her head high, which proved to be the wrong thing to do as a tear lost its moorings and slid down her cheek. Well, she supposed she did need something. She reached out and took a tissue. "Sorry."

"Don't be."

"I don't usually get so upset." She waved her hand in a vague way. "It's just because of—"

"It's okay," Conrad said and set the tissue box down on his desk.

"I've been fired." She didn't want him to think she was unhinged so she needed to explain there was a sensible reason for her tears. And she hadn't talked about the cancer with anyone since the one disastrous conversation with her boyfriend, so she wasn't going to mention that. "Well, technically not so much fired as not hired."

She took a breath.

"But I'm doing fine," she added before he could say anything more about the window washing job. "I have so much to be grateful for. Really."

"Yeah," he said in a voice almost as phony as hers.

He clearly didn't believe her. "Of course, I wasn't wild about having the muffler fall off. But my life is good," she said.

That might be a stretch. But she was at least trying to make everything right. After her surgery, she hadn't wanted to go back to her secretarial job, not when she craved so much more out of life. Over the years, she'd taken a dozen photography classes so she decided to at least try to make her dream come true.

Conrad looked up and glanced at the wall where a calendar hung. He was probably only checking the date, but Katrina's heart stopped.

"April 9," she offered quickly. "Today's Saturday, April 9."

She felt the heat rise on her face. She'd forgotten she was pictured on this month's page of that particular agricultural calendar. Last year, she'd answered an ad in the paper for models. She'd only wanted to see what a professional photo shoot was like, but she'd ended up being chosen to model for a Depression-era picture. The tractor was the star of the photo; she was in a distant farmhouse calling her "husband" home from the fields for dinner. She'd told herself she was far enough away that no one would recognize her.

Conrad looked up from his desk and opened his mouth to say something. Then he closed it again. He didn't say anything, but she noticed something had changed in his face. Maybe he was having a heart attack. He was white as snow. Well, not snow in general, but he sure matched the kind of gray that would be found in this town during winter. He was even slumped a little in his chair.

Just then the phone on his desk rang.

Conrad straightened himself and picked up the phone. "Service station. Nelson here."

Katrina could hear another man's voice indistinctly on the other end of the phone.

"Easy now," Conrad said as he put his hand over the receiver and looked up at her in apology. "Sorry, but this is my uncle. It'll only take a minute if—"

Katrina nodded. She was more than happy to leave. She turned and walked into the repair part of the gas station and shut the glass door behind her. She hadn't had a chance to tell Conrad that the car belonged to her sister, Leanne. Her sister had asked her, begged her really, to come for a visit. It had been bad timing, though. Katrina arrived at Leanne's place yesterday, just in time to listen to her sister fret about why her husband, Walker Rain Tree, hadn't come home the night before.

This morning, Leanne had asked her to take three-year-old Zach and six-year-old Ryan with her for the day so she and Walker could have a serious talk without them around. It seemed this wasn't the first night Leanne's husband had been gone and then refused to explain why. Katrina didn't want the boys to witness that kind of a quarrel either, so she said yes, and now the boys were asleep in the back of her sister's car. Leanne had insisted Katrina take her old car in case she wanted to take some of the back roads. That way, Katrina wouldn't risk damaging her leased Lexus.

On a whim, Katrina had promised the boys a quarter for each photo she took of them today. They had been excited about earning money so she expected they'd be up soon. Even with all of the delays, they should be home at Leanne's in time for an early dinner.

Conrad waited for the woman to walk out of his office before he put the phone back to his ear. "Now, start at the beginning."

He had to admit he was glad she was gone. His whole face relaxed. For a while he thought he might be hallucinating, but

his uncle Charley would bring him back
to reality.

"Is she still there?" the older man asked
a little unnecessarily in Conrad's opinion.
His uncle was looking out the window of
the hardware store across the street. There
was no way a person could leave Conrad's
gas station without being in full sight of
anyone looking out that window.

"Yeah, she's still here," he answered
anyway. "Did you happen to get a good
look at her?"

"Elmer said she has really long black hair
and is pretty."

A whole group of older men sat inside the
hardware store and kept their eyes on the
comings and goings of Dry Creek. Elmer had
underestimated her beauty, Conrad thought.
Pretty was too tame a word to describe her.
She was leggy and walked toward the beat-
up old car with her long hair swinging with
every step she took. She had warm brown
eyes and creamy skin. Even wearing jeans
and a black leather jacket, she was too exotic
for this place. He hadn't given much thought
to her apart from that until he saw the tears
in her eyes. That's when all of the pieces fell
into place and he recognized her.

Conrad remembered his uncle was waiting. "Yeah, she is that."

"Is she acting peculiar?"

"In what way?"

"Well, nervous. Is she anxious to get away from here?"

"She might be a little impatient, but lots of people are." He didn't know how to go about this, but he knew a man needed to lance a boil if he wanted it to heal. "The thing is she looks like someone in a picture I have and—"

"Aha," his uncle interrupted in triumph. "Elmer told me she's probably on one of those wanted posters you keep on that bulletin board of yours. The sheriff called and asked us to be on the lookout for an old gray car with a dent in the right fender. Somebody stole it down by Pryor. On the Crow Indian reservation. Even I could see her car is gray. And banged up, too."

Conrad closed his eyes. No one would steal that old car she was driving. Not unless they were drunk or too blind to see it clearly. "I don't think she's wanted for anything. That's not where I saw her." He drew a deep breath. "I know it's not her, but she looks like the woman on the calendar."

"What calendar?"

"You know the one I showed you."

There was a moment of absolute silence.

"You mean the woman you're going to marry?" Uncle Charley finally asked in a hushed tone. "That calendar?"

Conrad didn't know why he hadn't seen the pitfalls last week when he'd used a page in his calendar to make a point with his uncle. "No, she's not the woman I'm going to marry. I'm just saying—oh, I don't know what I'm saying."

The fact that he had not wanted to have a serious discussion with his uncle about his love life was the reason he was in trouble now. Last Wednesday the older man had come over to show Conrad what he'd put in the church prayer bulletin—"Wife wanted for my nephew."

A prayer didn't get more public than that. Or more embarrassing.

Conrad knew he should have sat down right there and assured his uncle that he would get married eventually, in his own time. But he was in the middle of rebuilding a tractor engine for the Redferns and they needed it soon if they were going to plow the ground they were leasing in time to get a crop planted. So he'd tried to stop his uncle's crusade the quick way, by pointing at the calendar on the wall and announcing that he had already picked out his future wife. It had been a joke, of course. Just a way to avoid the awkwardness of a conversation he didn't want to have.

"She's really here? Your *wife?*" His uncle sputtered, his voice rising.

"Don't get excited. It's not good for your blood pressure."

"Well, I can hardly believe it."

"That's because there's nothing to believe. It's just that someone who looks like the calendar woman is here."

When he said it out loud, it didn't sound so bad. The problem was Conrad wasn't sure this woman looked like anyone else. He'd never seen anyone like her in town before, not even when folks from the Miles City rodeo spilled over into the Dry Creek café. He took another look at her. For one thing, those strappy black high heels she wore would jump-start a dead man's heart. Women around here didn't wear shoes like that.

"Still, maybe it's a sign," Uncle Charley said hopefully.

"She just needs to get a new muffler on her car."

If he had to pick some woman to make his point, Conrad wondered why he hadn't chosen an ordinary woman who really existed in his world. Maybe someone like Tracy Stelling, who cut his hair once a month at the Quick Clips in Miles City. She'd grown up on one of the ranches near here and, although she'd left for a dozen or so years, she'd returned, looking subdued and grateful to be home. He'd have a chance with someone like that. He'd even been thinking of asking her out to dinner so he wouldn't be lying if he said he was considering Tracy for a wife.

"Every relationship needs to start someplace," his uncle said.

"That's the whole point. There is no relationship. She's just passing through. And she's not even the real woman. I mean the woman I thought she was."

He looked over at the calendar again. The woman was wearing a deep red dress with a white apron and holding open the door of a rundown farmhouse. The woman stood defiantly as if she was trying to fight off some crushing despair. He hadn't noticed until she was standing at his window, looking out and blinking back her tears, that her profile was the same as the calendar woman.

"Conrad? You still there?" his uncle asked.

He swallowed, but he couldn't talk. The calendar woman had reminded him of the feeling he'd had when he'd been five and his mother had died from pneumonia. Just the way she stood there holding that door, he'd known she'd shared the same feeling as him at some time in her life. They'd both screamed at the wind, even when no sound was coming out of their mouths.

"I'm just thinking—what if she did steal that car?" his uncle continued. "A thief could be dangerous. Knives. Guns. That kind of thing. Not that the sheriff said anything about the suspect being armed, but you never know. You need to be careful."

"Don't worry about me. I'm fine," Conrad said, hoping it was true.

"I could call the sheriff and have him check the woman out," his uncle persisted. "We should at least get a license plate number."

If it would make his uncle stop asking questions about the woman, he'd give him the numbers to Fort Knox if he had them.

He looked down at the work order he'd just filled out. "The plate number is SAQ718."

He'd had to go back into the service bay to write down the number because the woman didn't know it. Of course, lots of people didn't know their license plate numbers. That didn't mean they were driving stolen cars.

"Say it again so I can write it down."

"SAQ718. But I just don't think—"

"Well, you're a good judge of character," his uncle muttered, contradicting everything he'd said up to this point. "You're probably right about her. It wouldn't hurt to talk to her, though. Find out a little more about her."

"She's got two little kids in the backseat sleeping."

"Oh." His uncle's voice turned flat. "She's married then?"

To his surprise Conrad felt an echo of the older man's disappointment. He hadn't quite realized that. "I suppose that's what it means all right."

Now this, he told himself, was the reason it was foolish to put that prayer request out there. It was bound to be discouraging to everyone involved. He trusted God with his very soul, but when it came to finding a wife, all Conrad could remember were the few days in junior high when PE class became dance class. A boy, or a man, had to ask the question and hope for a dance even if he knew the woman would rather spit in his eye than say yes.

And the church—he couldn't bring the whole church congregation into this. There'd be advice given and awkward questions and, worst of all, expectations. No, a man needed to find his own wife. His friends couldn't do it for him.

"I've got to go," Conrad said in a hurry. "She's coming back over here."

"Now?" his uncle asked. "Hold on— I'll be there."

"No—She's my customer—I'll—" Ask her to dance, he almost said, but stopped himself.

"I'll bring her some coffee," his uncle said. "Don't worry about a thing."

"No—" Conrad protested again, but the phone was already dead.

He wasn't equipped for this kind of thing. He'd always figured that, if he married, it would be a dignified, orderly thing. If only he'd spoken directly to his uncle instead of making a joke, then he could have told him that he intended to ask Tracy out. He'd always thought that, if he got married, it would be to someone comfortable and safe like her.

He'd seen how his father had suffered when his mother died so he wasn't looking for some grand passion that would twist him around and knock him flat when something went wrong. He didn't expect his wife to be a great beauty or a great talker or to inspire a great feeling in him. She'd just be an average woman who was content to stand beside him in life.

He only had to look through the windows to see the calendar woman as she now stood waiting for him. There was nothing average about her.

Even more alarming, when he turned to look out the other window, he saw his uncle coming across the road with a grin on his weathered face and a cup of coffee in his hands. His arthritis certainly wasn't bothering him now.

Well, Conrad decided, there was nothing for him to do except to walk into the garage and find out what he was made of. She was waiting for him. It wasn't a good time for him to recollect that he never had learned to dance, but the thought came anyway. His palms were already starting to sweat.

Chapter Two

Katrina shivered as she crossed her arms and stood in place. The windows in here were small and covered with frost from last night. The smoke from the muffler still hung in the air. A large tractor took up half of the garage, but there was plenty of room for her to pace around her sister's old car.

"I'm freezing," she said as he was coming out of his office. She was surprised her nephews were warm enough with just their coats on to keep sleeping, but she'd checked on them and they were.

"The heat will kick on in a minute," Conrad said, stopping a few feet away from her. "I don't usually have customers back here so I don't keep it heated all the time. But I turned it up before I came through the door."

"Well, thanks." She drew her jacket closer.

It must be almost nine o'clock now and she'd left Leanne's place around six this morning. They both had been half-asleep then so she forgot to give Leanne the number for her cell phone. Not that she would have expected to hear from her sister anyway. Walker hadn't come home until early morning and Leanne said he would sleep late. Katrina had been careful not to comment on Walker's absence. It didn't matter how suspicious it looked to her, Leanne needed to be the one to decide if her husband might be unfaithful.

"There's a bulletin board over there that has some jobs listed on it." Conrad pointed to the far wall. "It's mostly cleaning houses, but you might find something to do until you get a more regular job."

Just then a beam of morning light made its way through the frost on the window and settled on Conrad's head, gradually showing up the sprinkling of golden strands in his brown hair. Now that was the kind of diffused light she'd wanted for her photographs. She didn't know why she wasn't rushing to get her camera. The longer she looked at Conrad the more of a glow he had. And his green eyes were filled with the mossy colors found in a backwoods pond. Even his skin was taking on a rosier hue. The faint roughness of whiskers on his cheeks and the set of his jaw made him look rugged and strong.

It was unusual that sunlight would make that much difference. He was almost handsome.

"You didn't get into your wife's shampoo, did you?" Katrina asked before she thought about it. "Your hair sparkles."

"There's no wife. I got some grease on my head working under that tractor." He nodded to the piece of equipment standing in his garage. "My aunt Edith made up something with lemon juice and other things to get it out. I smelled like fruit pie for days."

So, he was single. "Well, it works. Your hair is great."

Then she remembered she shouldn't be asking any man if he was single. Not until she knew whether or not her cancer was coming back. She didn't need a repeat of the scene with her boyfriend when he decided being with someone who was sick was not sufficiently entertaining to keep him by her side.

Conrad's face eased up a fraction. "Thanks. If you need anything, just let me know."

He seemed to mean it which surprised her enough that she considered telling him all her troubles just to see if he was like her ex-boyfriend. It wasn't easy to tell someone, though.

She hadn't even told Leanne about the cancer. At first, she hadn't wanted to worry her and then, when the surgery was all over, she didn't know how to say the words. Maybe later, when Leanne wasn't so worried about her marriage, she'd tell her then. If she waited a few months, she'd know more anyway. By then she hoped to be closer to her sister, too.

"Is it getting warmer in here?" Conrad asked.

She nodded.

He was looking at her again with concern, only this time he didn't seem to be worried that she was going to fall apart. "My uncle is coming over."

"That's nice."

"Well," he said without much enthusiasm. "He won't stay long."

They were both silent for a minute.

"He'll probably ask if you ever had your picture taken for a calendar."

Katrina swallowed. "Oh. So you did notice?"

The director for the ad had kept pressing her to feel the despair of that woman caught in a never-ending drought. Finally, Katrina had let her emotions go.

Conrad nodded.

"Well, it was a mistake." When Katrina saw the final picture, she was appalled. The camera had caught her emotions too well. "I never thought about all those people looking at me. All month long. It's strange."

"I can understand that," he said.

He stood and looked over her shoulder at the tractor.

"I didn't mean I don't like people to look at me in person." She wondered how neurotic he thought she was.

"Oh." He looked back at her. This time he smiled. "Good."

He shuffled his feet. "If you need anything, let me know."

"I could use some juice," Katrina said. Every time she saw that calendar she got thirsty. "For the boys when they wake up. They've been sleeping a long time. Is there a place I can get some?"

"There's a vending machine in the back."

He motioned to the far corner of the garage. "It has some boxes of apple juice. If you need some quarters, let me know."

She looked and saw the bright blue machine with the red stripes along the rear wall of his shop.

"I've got plenty of change in my purse," Katrina said. She'd left her purse in the car and when she turned in that direction she saw a small head in the window.

"Looks like they're waking up," Conrad said as he followed her gaze and waved at Ryan. "Do they sleep in the car like this often?"

"I don't know. I haven't taken them anywhere before."

His face went white. "But they're yours, right?"

She shook her head. "They're used to the car, though. They probably sleep in it all the time so they're fine."

He was silent. Maybe even stunned. He certainly didn't have that friendly expression on his face anymore.

Just then she heard the side door open to the garage. She looked up and a gray-haired man stepped inside holding a coffee cup. Short and a little stout, he had a red shirt on his back and his hair was puffed up around him like he'd been in a windstorm. Even his cheeks were rosy.

"Maybe you should go back and get another cup," Conrad said to the old man as he stood in the doorway with the cup held out. "Tell Elmer he might be right about ev-erything. That's ev-ery-thing."

Conrad's voice was funny. Each word was spoken clearly before the other word came out of his mouth. Maybe his uncle had trouble hearing.

"Oh," the old man said as he looked into the garage like he was trying to find something.

Through the open door, Katrina could see that the sky was darker than when she'd seen it last. It was probably going to rain or snow before long. There were no more beams of sunlight sneaking through.

"Let me just give the coffee to your friend here. No point in taking it back," the older man said as he stepped into the garage and looked straight at Katrina. "Hello. I'm Charley Nelson."

She moved closer to save him some steps. It was brave of him to meet new people when he obviously had challenges.

"Let—me—help—you," she said carefully and a bit louder than Conrad. Then she reached out to take the cup. "Thank you for bringing me some coffee. I'm Katrina Britton."

The older man seemed startled, but he gave her the cup. Then he stood there grinning.

Conrad spoke up then. "It seems the boys aren't hers. I'm guessing the car might not be, either."

She turned and saw he looked upset.

"Well, not everyone has children," she protested. She didn't know what business that was of Conrad's. And who cared about the car? "That doesn't mean we can't enjoy being around someone else's children. I was just taking them for a ride."

The old man must have agreed, because he didn't even talk about children when he said, "I'm sorry. I didn't know if you liked cream or sugar so I just brought it black."

He probably hadn't heard Conrad, she concluded. The poor man. It must be hard to carry on a conversation.

"Black—is—fine," she said loudly and took the cup. Then she pointed to her ear. "I—understand."

That seemed to delight him.

"My uncle Charley hears fine," Conrad

said from behind her. "He's just being stubborn."

"How can you say that? He brought me coffee in a beautiful mug." She looked down at the red cup she held. It had a white heart and a winged figure. "Why it's a cupid mug!"

"Love is always in the air around here." The older man stepped closer to her, still grinning.

"Love isn't all that's in the air," Conrad muttered. He didn't sound too happy. "Bonnie and Clyde were in love. That didn't mean you'd want them to come to your town. Or take your children for rides in your car."

Katrina took a sip of the coffee. It was good and strong.

"We're known for our love matches in this town," Charley continued, not looking at his nephew. "We even have a stop sign that's shaped like a heart up the road a bit. It got bent like that years ago when a couple of teenagers—one of them my son, actually—had an accident while they were eloping. It's our main tourist attraction."

"We don't have any tourists," Conrad protested.

Katrina certainly could believe that.

"You need to put on Shakespearean plays or something. Or build a water park. They're popular."

"We're a good, decent town. That should be enough," Conrad said.

Then it struck her. She turned to the old man. "You have a stop sign shaped like a heart?"

"Well, half a heart," he admitted. "It's where the fender of my old pickup hit it."

She set her cup of coffee on the roof of her sister's car.

"That'd be perfect." She used her hands to try and picture that sign. Maybe she wasn't out of the running to supply photos for that Romance Across America calendar after all. She'd already used most of her savings hiring those models for the photos she'd sent. She'd had beautiful blonde women and men with teeth so white they gleamed. But maybe she could find a couple of models that would work for some kind of future payment. She had her camera in the trunk. She had film. If she could get strong enough natural daylight, she'd have a chance.

"Do you have any blondes here?" she continued. "You know, young women in their twenties who'd like to take a chance at modeling. Pretty, of course, and curvy—"

Well, maybe not too many curves, she thought. Her boyfriend had been swayed by the curves of one of the models as much as he had been by Katrina's surgery. She'd only had a partial mastectomy, but he said it made him uncomfortable. The young blonde, on the other hand, apparently made him very comfortable.

"Curvy? Why?" Conrad sounded bewildered.

She eyed him skeptically.

"I want to take some pictures. I guess the main thing is that the models have fresh faces and lots of heart," she finally said. "They need to look sincere when they pretend to be in love. I often tell my models to think of food when they're trying to look smitten."

Uncle Charley's face brightened. "That's a tip we can all live by. I love my wife's cooking. Especially her sour cream raisin pie. Every time Edith bakes it, I fall in love with her all over again."

Just then there was the sound of a siren in the distance. Katrina saw Conrad's jaw tighten.

"Elmer called in the number before I left," the older man said with a quick look at her. "I didn't wait to hear what the sheriff said, but I guess they matched since he's here."

"Sheriff?" Katrina asked. "What's wrong?"

Conrad knew there was no need to go over and open the door. Sheriff Carl Wall would find his way into the garage. His uncle had just been making sure the woman stayed here, Conrad concluded. That made sense, thankfully.

Meanwhile, the woman had moved closer to the car so Conrad stepped around to block her. He didn't know who those two boys were, but he didn't want her to use them as hostages.

Suddenly, it occurred to him. "They're not drugged, are they?"

"Who?" The woman turned bewildered eyes to him.

"The boys."

He wondered if she would play the innocent until the end. He'd sure been fooled by her. He'd never tell anyone, but after seeing her tears he had been planning to put a new muffler on that old car of hers and not charge her a dime. Wouldn't that have been something?

The door to the garage opened and Sheriff Wall stepped inside. He pushed his worn Stetson back so he could see from beneath the brim. He was a solid man and he didn't put up with much nonsense from people. He got his hair cut by Tracy in Miles City, too, so underneath his hat he was neatly, but conservatively, trimmed.

"Conrad," the sheriff said with a nod. Then he turned his head slightly and nodded again, "Charley."

He looked at Katrina. "Ma'am."

The sheriff had a gray wool jacket over his uniform and Conrad realized he was relieved the man hadn't come in with his guns drawn. Catching a car thief would be high excitement for the sheriff, but he seemed to be taking it in stride.

"What do we have here?" the sheriff asked in a mild voice as he stepped behind the car so he could see the license plate.

"I'm sure the plates are current," Katrina said. "They have the sticker on them for this year."

If Katrina had stolen that car, she was

good. Conrad had to give her that. She sounded like a concerned motorist. But the sheriff needed to know everything wasn't the way it looked.

"She's got two boys in the backseat," Conrad said. "She doesn't know them."

"I didn't say I don't know them," Katrina protested. "I said they're not mine."

"So you're not married?" Charley asked.

"What difference does it make?" she asked in surprise. "A woman doesn't need a husband to drive a car."

Charley just beamed, his wrinkled face all scrunched up with a smile. Conrad knew what his uncle was thinking and he didn't like it.

"So is she the thief?" Conrad decided it was time to bring everyone back down to earth.

"Well, it is a bit early to be making accusations," the sheriff said. He walked around the car and looked in the windows.

"What's going on here?" Katrina demanded.

The sheriff shrugged. "We'll know soon. I have a call in to the officials on the Crowe reservation. They take care of their own problems. I don't have jurisdiction there. I'm just looking into this as a professional courtesy."

"What problems?" Katrina asked. "Is something wrong with Leanne?"

Conrad looked over and saw two heads staring out of the car. "Both boys are up now."

"Well, why don't I have a little chat with them and see what they say," the sheriff said as he turned to look in the car windows. Then he turned back to Conrad. "It might be best if you took the young lady into your office while I talk to the boys."

Conrad nodded. "Makes sense."

"And make sure she doesn't make any phone calls," the sheriff added. "She might be working with someone."

"I'm not working with anyone," Katrina protested. "I mean, I didn't do anything either so I don't need a partner."

The sheriff grunted and looked at Charley. "Why don't you go with them, too?"

Conrad could see that Katrina wanted to protest, but she didn't. Instead, she walked ahead of him with her head held high and that long hair of hers swinging again like she was some princess. Her back was straight with indignation.

And, as if that wasn't bad enough, Uncle

Charley leaned over and whispered, "Did you hear that? She's single."

Conrad muttered low enough that only Charley could hear. "Give it up. We've got trouble enough."

He couldn't stop watching her, though. Her high heels didn't even wobble as she marched across the concrete floor. Which was more than he could say for his heart. He supposed it was only natural that, after he'd looked at that calendar a hundred times over the past week, he would feel some warmth for the woman in the picture. He had sense enough to know that had nothing to do with real life though. This woman could be a criminal.

The three of them had no sooner stepped into his office than Katrina turned on them.

"Are you going to tell me what's going on?" she demanded. Her hands were on her hips and the color was high on her face.

Conrad didn't figure it was the time to say she looked magnificent.

His uncle wasn't so sensitive. "My!"

Fortunately, the older man didn't elaborate, but Conrad recognized the appreciation anyway.

"The sheriff got a call," Conrad answered.

He figured she deserved to know. "The car you're driving was reported stolen."

"That car belongs to my sister. She lent it to me so I could go out scouting around for places that look romantic."

"You mean like our stop sign?" Conrad asked in astonishment.

Uncle Charley just stood there looking like a cat who'd found a bowl of cream. "Romance?"

"If you must know, I'm hoping to become a professional photographer. I took some shots for a calendar called Romance Across America. I am—well, was—looking for locations for photo shoots this morning."

The fire went out of her as she spoke.

"That's the job you lost?" Conrad asked softly.

She nodded. "I'm thinking I could make another pitch for it, but I've already sent them my best work so I don't know. They said my pictures lacked heart."

"What do they know?" Conrad said without thinking. He wasn't ready to champion this woman. True, something about her tugged at him. But he had sense enough to know that she would break his heart if he let himself get involved with her.

"So you're a professional photographer?" Uncle Charley asked. "That's why you wanted someone to stand by our heart sign?"

Katrina nodded.

"Then young lady, that makes you an answer to prayer," he said with satisfaction in his voice.

"What?" Conrad almost swallowed his tongue. Here he was trying to be sensible and his uncle was diving off the deep end. Surely, there had to be a limit to what his relatives would do in pursuit of a bride for him. "I'm sure you don't mean—"

"No, she's an answer to prayer." Uncle Charley was adamant. He turned to Katrina. "My wife, Edith, has been praying up a storm asking God to send us a photographer to take some pictures for the church directory. She's set on us having photos now that the church in Miles City has them. She says we need to keep up with the times."

"The church directory?" Conrad was so relieved he didn't care that he sounded like a simple-minded parrot.

"I don't really—" Katrina stammered. "That is, I mean, I really should keep looking for more—well, other work. I used to be a secretary. I suppose I could do that again."

Conrad saw all the life leave her face.

"We've got money to pay for the directory pictures," Uncle Charley said.

"I don't work for churches," Katrina said. "I don't even go inside them."

Conrad could hear the bitterness in her voice. He expected his uncle to concede defeat. There might be a prayer request in the church bulletin asking for a wife for him, but no one would suggest he marry a woman who wasn't at peace with God. That would be unending trouble. Instead of dropping the subject, though, his uncle got a thoughtful look on his face.

"I'll help you find a blonde for that picture you want of the heart sign," the older man bargained. "All you have to do is help my wife set up the directory. Give her some pointers. Maybe take a few photos for starters. And you've got yourself a model."

"But I—"

"You don't need to set foot inside the church if you don't want. And I'll get you the best-looking blonde in Dry Creek."

"Really?" Katrina asked. Her face glowed. "That heart sign is perfect."

Conrad didn't know how a post of rusted

metal could move a woman from despair to happiness, but it sure looked like one had.

Uncle Charley nodded. "It's a deal then."

Conrad's heart sank. He loved his uncle and didn't want to see him get hurt. But no good could come from being so friendly to a woman who showed up in a stolen car. He'd make sure the church didn't give her any advance money in the hopes she would take the directory job.

The woman walked over to the window. "Can I see the sign from here?"

"Just look down the road to your left as far as you can see," Uncle Charley told her.

"I see that garden gnome," she said without glancing back at them. She was quiet for a second. "Then the church. You know your church could use a steeple."

"We're looking into it," Charley said. "It takes money, though. And we have the directory to do. We're a small church."

She turned back. "I'm not taking all those pictures. Just so you know. I'm willing to get your wife started and do a few for examples, but that's it."

Charley nodded and she turned back to the window.

"I don't see it," Katrina said.

"You're looking in the right direction. It's farther down," his uncle answered.

She moved her head, straining even more to locate it.

Conrad started to wonder if she wasn't trying to figure the fastest way out of town instead of looking for that sign. Or maybe she was just searching for a place to hide. If so, it'd be difficult. Most of the houses had fences around them, but all of them were see-through bars or wire so they wouldn't conceal much. There weren't any leaves on any of the bushes so she couldn't hide in the shrubbery, either.

"The doors are all locked around here," he said. That was an exaggeration. Granted, most of the front doors would be because no one wanted to track the mud and snow of early spring into their living rooms. But the back doors would be unlocked. That's where the rugs and boots were kept. He'd hate to have anyone come up against a car thief just because they didn't know one was in town, though.

Katrina turned to look at him in puzzlement. "I don't need doors for the photos. Just the sign."

Conrad grunted. She sure seemed innocent. "I'm just saying."

She gave him a look and turned back to the window.

By now he figured he didn't have to worry about being drawn into her web. The expression on her face said she wasn't planning to cozy up to him anytime soon, either. Well, he supposed it was for the best.

He took a few steps farther away from her.

His uncle walked over and leaned closer to him. "You could be a little nicer. She might be your calendar lady."

His uncle's voice was low and Katrina couldn't hear them.

"She *is* the calendar lady," Conrad said.

"Really? Then that means—"

"It means nothing. I was joking when I said what I did. There's no miracle answer to prayer going on here."

"But—"

Conrad ignored his uncle. "The fact is, I've been thinking I should ask Tracy at the Quick Clip in Miles City out to dinner."

"Really? Linda at the diner said you two might make a couple."

Conrad nodded. He was glad to see

someone else had some sense. "We'd be comfortable together."

"Comfortable?" Uncle Charley exclaimed with a frown.

Katrina turned around and looked at them in puzzlement.

"Nothing's wrong," Conrad said to her and she went back to her window

Then he turned to his uncle and said in a low voice, "Yes. Safe and comfortable."

They were both silent for a minute.

"It's my fault you're willing to settle for that," Uncle Charley said, his voice upset. "I should have paid more attention to you when your mother died. I didn't know your father was so wrapped up in his grief he wasn't even home most of the time."

"We got by."

"Yes, but—"

"I do okay," Conrad said. He could hardly even talk about those days after his mother died. Some things were just better left unsaid. There was no undoing what happened anyway.

The older man nodded and started to walk away.

Conrad didn't mean to upset his uncle. The man was only trying to help him out.

Just then it struck him. "Why, you don't even know any young blondes to use in the picture of that sign. How are you going to find a model?"

His uncle winked at him. "I figure that's your department."

"My—" Conrad was speechless. How was he supposed to find a pretty blonde willing to pose by an old stop sign?

No one said anything for a moment.

"It could be she's innocent," his uncle finally added with a nod toward the window. "Just like she says. I'd hate to think we treated her unfairly in Dry Creek if she is. God wants us to do better than that."

Conrad didn't have a chance to answer because just then Katrina stepped back from the window. She was beaming.

"I think I saw it," she said.

Conrad sighed. His uncle was right. He needed to see that she was given the benefit of the doubt. If for no other reason than that she was still his customer. He'd built his business on doing everything he could for his customers. Usually, that didn't include standing beside them as they were arrested, of course, but he would do what he could. Besides, seeing her with her face lit up touched him somehow. No wonder he'd been willing to put a two-hundred-dollar muffler on her car and not charge her for it. The woman was a wonder. Well, either that or a very good actress. He wished he knew which it was.

Chapter Three

Katrina turned around and looked through the window into the garage. Fifteen more minutes had passed and the sheriff was still talking to the boys. She hadn't noticed until now, but someone had turned on a radio and a big band tune was playing softly. She saw the radio sitting on a green file cabinet behind the desk. She hadn't heard the soft static of a radio in years. It must have been Conrad's uncle who thought of the music since he was standing over there looking pleased with himself.

She looked up at the older man's lined face. "Thanks. Dance music always cheers me up."

She tapped her hands against her leg in time to the music just to show him she was feeling better.

The old man's face lit up. "I had a hunch you might be a dancer. Conrad dances, too, you know."

Katrina heard a garbled sound over by the door. Conrad had his hands in his pockets and a look of panic on his face. She half expected him to open the door and rush outside to check the gas pumps, but he didn't.

"In junior high," he muttered to her instead and then gave a dark look to his uncle. "I don't dance now."

"It's like riding a bicycle," the old man said as he bobbed his head to the beat of the music. "It'll come back to you."

"I fell off my bicycle. Remember?"

"Well, at first, but you got the hang of it," his uncle said and then paused. "Later."

Katrina wondered if dance moves did come back. "I took some ballet in junior high."

Conrad shot her a look of pure terror. "I could never do ballet."

"Nonsense," his uncle said. "You got back on that bike until you could ride it. And you suited up as a clown at the last rodeo. That takes more nerve than ballet."

"I only did it because the real clown didn't show and the riders needed someone to be in the ring with them in case they needed help."

"So you'd risk your life to help an old cowboy," his uncle said. "But when it comes to bringing a little pleasure into a beautiful woman's heart, you fold."

"Well, I suppose I could dance if someone's life was on the line," Conrad conceded.

"You never know what you can do until you have to," Katrina agreed. She knew the two men were trying to keep her mind off her troubles and she appreciated it.

"I ran into a burning building once," Conrad offered. "Never thought I'd be able to do that. It was more of a shed than anything, but—"

His face had more color now that they'd stopped talking about dancing.

"That was a fool thing to do," his uncle scolded. "That old cat never did appreciate it. She scratched you up good. You could have gotten an infection."

"Well, she'd gotten tangled up in some string and couldn't get out. I couldn't just let her die, now could I?"

"No, I suppose not," his uncle agreed. "I've done reckless things, too. I can remember when I went skinny-dipping at the church picnic when we all used to meet at the Big Dry Creek. I was a young daredevil of seven and I thought I was far enough away. Almost didn't get my clothes on before some ladies came down to see how high the water was in the creek. And there I stood dripping wet in my shirt and pants. Looked like a fool."

No one said anything for a bit.

"I never thought I'd have the courage to face getting arrested," Katrina finally added to the list. "But here I am."

She looked around. Everything in the office was neatly squared off, the stack of invoices on the desktop. The white binders named with different motor companies. Even the way the file cabinets were arranged. The place was pleasantly warm, too, and she had one friend here. Conrad's uncle seemed to believe she was innocent.

"That sheriff won't arrest you," the older man muttered. "He has to stand for reelection in this town. I guess he could hold you for a few days, though."

"It's okay," she said. "He's only doing his job,"

Then the door from the garage opened and

the sheriff came into the office. "I'm sorry. That took longer than I thought it would."

He didn't close the door to the garage area.

"Are the boys okay?" she asked as she stepped over to try and see them. The lights were off in the garage and only the subdued sunlight that filtered through the windows made it possible to see. The boys were sitting inside the car again. She could see the tops of their little heads.

The sheriff nodded. "Yeah, they're doing fine. That older one's pretty sharp."

Katrina had no choice but to turn back and look at the lawman even if she wasn't ready. He had a stern look on his face and it made her think he was expecting the worst. Well, she was expecting something pretty awful, too. And it would be happening to her, not him.

She didn't see Conrad take a few steps closer to her, but she heard him. She looked up and saw him standing next to her with the same resolve in his face as the lawman had on his. Only Conrad was directing his glare toward the sheriff instead of her.

She took a deep breath. Maybe she had two friends to stand beside her.

"It could be that the plates are stolen," she

said to the sheriff. She tried to keep her voice from pleading. "Maybe the car thieves took Leanne's plates and put stolen ones on her car just to confuse things."

"It could have happened that way," Conrad said.

The sheriff raised his eyebrow in surprise and looked at Conrad for a second before bringing his eyes back to her. "Those boys said you promised them money if they'd come with you today. Did you cross any state lines?"

"No, and I was only going to give them quarters. One for each picture I took with them in it."

She tried to smile at the sheriff.

He didn't return the courtesy. "The oldest one seems to think he'll have enough money to buy something called a Guzmoo or Gazmoo. Sounded like a military tank."

"It's a video game and I assure you he isn't going to make that much."

Katrina realized that might not make her look good, either, so she added, "I never told him he'd make enough for one of those things. He just got carried away. Besides, they're my nephews. My sister's boys."

"The sister with the car?" the sheriff asked.

She nodded. "Leanne Britton. Well, Rain Tree now. She's married to—"

"Walker Rain Tree," the sheriff filled in with a nod. "He sent word through a friend that the car was stolen. Walker lives down on the Crowe reservation. I've seen him here and there. Used to work construction in Miles City. Big guy."

Katrina had only met her brother-in-law once and that was before Leanne married him, but she didn't want to bring that up right now. She couldn't imagine why he'd report that Leanne's car was stolen. Or why Leanne hadn't stopped him.

"Jobs have been hard to find," Katrina said. "My sister says he hasn't worked much in the past year."

"That's got to be difficult," the sheriff said, studying Katrina. "You got employment somewhere yourself?"

Conrad stepped so close she could feel his arm next to hers. "Having a job—not having a job. It's not a crime."

Katrina was glad to have Conrad beside her.

The sheriff looked at Conrad again, his eyes narrowing this time. "I thought you didn't know this woman."

"He doesn't," Katrina said. "He just worries about justice being done and—" She waved vaguely. "Things in general."

The lawman grunted. "That's Conrad, all right."

Then the sheriff turned his attention back to her. "These boys, they don't seem too sure about you. They say they just met you yesterday. Aunts usually know their nephews, at least by the time they're six."

She heard censure in his voice.

"Well, I've been busy. And, my sister and I have had our problems." She looked at the sheriff. She didn't want to say those problems involved Walker. Katrina had opposed the marriage and her sister hadn't forgiven her. That didn't have anything to do with the car anyway. "We really just need to call my sister and straighten this all out. Like I said, these probably aren't even her license plates."

"Since Walker is the one who had someone report the car as stolen, I need to clear it with him," the sheriff said. "You've got the phone number?"

"Of course," Katrina said. "It's the house number. Neither one of them have cell phones. But my purse is in the car and the number is in there on an old receipt. I'll get it for you."

"I'd rather have someone else bring your purse out of the car," the sheriff said. "If you don't mind, that is?"

Katrina got the feeling it didn't matter if she minded or not.

"I'll get it," Uncle Charley said as he walked over to the open door leading to the garage.

"There's some sandwiches in the front seat," Katrina called out to him as he walked through the doorway. "Those boys are probably hungry. Tell them I'll bring them some juice in a minute or two."

She hoped the sheriff noticed that she was trying to take care of her nephews.

"I'll bring you your coffee back, too," the older man said from inside the garage.

"Those boys will want a hot meal," Conrad said quietly beside her. "When we finish here, I'll take the three of you to the café for breakfast. My treat."

Katrina felt her eyes grow damp again. Really, this man was being very nice.

Then Conrad said, "The sheriff can't take you to jail until someone comes for the boys anyway. If he can't reach the parents, he'd have to call Children's Services in Billings."

Well, that was an effective douse of cold water, Katrina thought, as she stepped away to look up at her betrayer. Instead of having his eyes aimed at her, though, Conrad had them focused on the sheriff.

It was clear from the twist to the sheriff's mouth that he hadn't given any thought to what would happen to the boys if he arrested Katrina. Of course, she knew Leanne would be over here in a few hours once they called her, but the sheriff didn't.

He just stood there.

"I don't think I've ever arrested someone who had kids with them," the lawman finally said. "I wasn't really planning to put her in jail right now anyway. At least not without checking out her story. We have to pay Miles City for room and board every time we give them a prisoner. It adds up."

"Don't worry, Leanne will vouch for me," Katrina said and then stopped. It had already occurred to her that Leanne and Walker might be off somewhere together. Or maybe they'd had a fight and that's why Walker said the car was stolen. Maybe Leanne was in the Lexus and Walker in his pickup. Either way, they might not get back to answer the phone until late tonight.

"The children seem to check out," the sheriff conceded. "And I'm not keen to pay Children's Services. Travel. Meals. And they always take their time. We're over our budget as it is."

Conrad pressed his point. "Then while you make your calls, you won't object to me taking Katrina and the boys to the café for something to eat?"

The sheriff shrugged. "It's your dime."

"I can pay," Katrina said.

"Don't let her convince you to let her go free, either." This command was given to Conrad. "That'd be a mistake."

"Of course not," Conrad said. "I'm just doing what needs being done."

Katrina tried not to let that sting. She should know he was only doing his duty by her. He probably had something in his code of honor that said he had to stand by any weeping women who faced the law in his gas station. She couldn't worry about that now, though.

"And be sure she doesn't call anyone on that phone of hers," the sheriff continued.

She reached into the pocket of her jacket

and pulled out her cell phone. "Here. It's not even on. Keep it if you need to."

The sheriff took it and put it in his own pocket. "It's just until I check things out."

Then she saw Charley start walking back from the car. He had her purse in one hand and her youngest nephew, Zach, in the other. Her older nephew, Ryan, was following behind them.

The boys were looking a little scared.

She glanced up at the sheriff. "There's no need to talk about arresting me in front of my nephews. They don't need to be any more upset than they are."

The sheriff snorted. "The only reason they might be upset is that they think I'm going to stop you from giving them their quarters. That's what they wanted to know about. Besides I wouldn't talk about arresting anyone in front of their kids if I could help it. Or even just holding them for questioning, either."

"Well," Katrina said with a nod. "I appreciate that."

"I'm not the bad guy," the sheriff added. But he still held his hand out for her purse when Charley brought it in the office.

"I can open my own purse," she said.

"Got to check it out for—you know," he said with a meaningful look at her nephews.

Which, of course, stopped her protest. She didn't want him getting specific.

Instead, she smiled at the boys. "Everything's all right."

Both boys were still frowning.

"Of course it is," Conrad added with enough confidence that the boys relaxed.

The sky was spitting rain by the time Conrad grabbed his jacket and got everyone ready to go over to the café. Uncle Charley had already gone ahead and the sheriff was sitting outside in his car filling out paperwork. The lawman hadn't gotten an answer when he called the number on the back of that receipt. Conrad figured the man couldn't finish his report until he at least talked to Leanne and Walker, though.

Conrad put the Closed sign on his door.

"What if someone needs you?" Katrina asked when she saw what he'd done. "You can't just close your business in the middle of the day. You're the only gas station here."

He shrugged. "The pumps work with a credit card. And everyone knows to look for me at the café if they really need help and I'm not around here."

Katrina shook her head. "This isn't how it's done in Los Angeles."

"I expect not," Conrad agreed as he opened the door. So that's where she lived.

Conrad took a deep breath when he stepped outside. The air smelled of damp earth and the sky was dark gray. There'd be no more sunshine today. He had only one umbrella so he turned and gave that to Katrina. Little boys never minded rain.

"My mom says we can't walk in the mud unless she says it is okay," Ryan announced after he stepped out the door. The tin roof of Conrad's shop covered the concrete slab around the gas pumps, too, but the area beyond that was getting wet.

"Walk on the road," Conrad said. Katrina and the youngest boy had come out behind Ryan and waited on the slab. "There's no mud on the asphalt."

"Maybe we could go off the road a little," Ryan suggested hopefully as he stepped to the edge of the pavement. "I can carry my shoes so they won't get dirty. I see a worm out there."

Katrina turned around. "You don't want

to get the floor of the café all muddy when we go to breakfast."

Conrad laughed. What boy that age was worried about a floor? "That worm is long gone. Besides, you'll have to keep your feet and your shoes clean if you want your aunt to take your picture. Your clothes, too."

"Oh," Ryan said with a nod. "I guess so."

Conrad kept his hand on the boy's shoulder as he led the way to the café. "People don't really take that many pictures around here. We're too close to the Black Hills, I guess. They get more striking pictures there."

"Are we going there, Aunt Kat-rr—" Ryan gave up on the name and just looked up at her. The boy seemed anxious and Conrad watched him carefully as he continued. "You're still going to take our pictures, aren't you?"

Conrad relaxed. The boy just wanted his quarters. He was greedy, not afraid.

"I hope so, sweetie," Katrina said softly as she guided Zach down the street.

She held the umbrella over her head, but the rain slanted in sideways and Conrad could see that her hair was getting damp. He hoped her black jacket didn't get too wet.

Her jeans would survive a soaking, but the leather looked imported. She had probably gotten it at Rodeo Drive down in Beverly Hills. He was getting ready to caution her to be careful of the rain, when she stepped over a crack in the asphalt in her high heels and he forgot all about the weather.

He almost had to stop and catch his breath again. The sight of those black patent leather straps wrapped around her delicate ankles made him think of the grand Hollywood movie stars of old like Marilyn Monroe. Those shoes of Katrina's were all steam and sizzle. He hoped that none of the ranch hands from the Elkton place were at the café. They'd scc those shoes as an invitation to flirt shamelessly. She even had her toenails painted a deep red. He'd never seen feet look so pretty in the rain.

"I have some boots you can borrow," he said.

Katrina turned around, a stricken expression on her face. "You're right. I can't go to pri—" she stopped herself. "I couldn't go with the sheriff in my high heels. I meant to put tennis shoes in the trunk, but they're in my car—not my sister's."

"They're nice shoes," Conrad felt obliged

to say. He wasn't the kind of man to be taken in by nice footwear, however. He hoped that, if there were any ranch hands at the café, they didn't decide to help her get out of town before the sheriff got all his information. Some of them would do that for a woman wearing shoes like that.

They finished walking down the road together.

"Nice place," Katrina said as they started walking up the steps to the café porch. There was an overhang so rain wasn't hitting them where they stood. Katrina lowered her umbrella and shook it out. Ryan was already up to the door and Zach was holding on to Katrina's leg.

"I'll carry the umbrella in for you," Conrad said, but all he did was stand there looking at her. He told himself he was making sure no one could tell she was suspected of a crime before they went inside. He didn't know what clues he was looking for, though.

Strands of Katrina's hair were wet and hanging down. She was no longer as perfect as she had been when she drove into his gas station and he liked her better for it. Drops of rain glistened on her cheeks. Her eyes were warm and a little shy.

If this were one of those old Hollywood movies, Conrad decided he would be saying something romantic about now. He tried to make the notion go away, but it lingered in his mind. It was just that all of the talk lately about him getting married was stirring around in his mind. He needed to put it to rest. She certainly wasn't the kind of woman he intended to become involved with. He already knew she was trouble. She cried. She liked old bent-up signs. She shouted to make herself heard by an old man she thought was deaf. She drank cold coffee. He wanted to like his wife, not love her. He'd learned how much love could hurt when his mother died. Katrina was just too intense for him.

And she had rain dripping down her cheeks. He reached out and wiped a drop away.

"It's not another tear," she said. "I was just caught by surprise earlier. I'm really not that much of a crybaby."

Another raindrop slid down her cheek and he caught that one, too. Her skin was cool and smooth like polished marble. "You had cause."

She seemed surprised at that. He winced.

He had no business saying something like that. He needed to bury his emotions. For all he knew, she could be lying about her sister—and the car. She might not be striving to be a photographer or a good aunt. She might even have known he was the kind of guy to give away a new muffler to someone who couldn't pay for it. She might be playing him for an old fool.

"Hey, who are those people?" Ryan interrupted as he stepped between them.

Conrad looked at where they boy was pointing. And there they were. Half a dozen faces were gathered around the front window of the café, shamelessly watching him and Katrina through the glass. He could call them out by name. Elmer. Uncle Charley. Aunt Edith. Linda Enger, the owner of the café. Pete Denning who worked at the Elkton ranch. And, the most surprising one of all, Tracy. What was she doing here? She lived in Miles City.

"Do you know those people?" Katrina asked.

By now, half of the people on the café side of the window were waving and smiling at them, trying to make it seem like they were just being friendly. Linda and Tracy weren't looking so happy, but, smiling or not, he could hardly disown any of them.

"Unfortunately, yes. I know them," he said and, with that, he stepped over and opened the door.

"We've been expecting you," Linda said as she came over to the entry. Her voice was cool when she said it, though, which was unusual for her. "Charley just told us you were on your way here."

"Good," Conrad said. Why did she make it sound like Charley had warned them? Surely, Charley hadn't said anything about the car being stolen. He noticed Linda hadn't taken the good silverware off her tables so she couldn't be too worried about theft.

Linda held out two menus. "Welcome."

"Your place is beautiful," Katrina said as she took one of the menus and looked around. "Are those antiques on the wall?"

Linda stiffened. "They're just family items. Nothing valuable."

"They've been hanging there forever," Conrad added. "No resale value at all."

Well, maybe Linda did know about the car. He didn't think there was any cause for concern, though. The old memorabilia hanging on the walls was there to add to the fifties look of the café. He knew the guitar on the left side had belonged to Linda's husband, Duane, when he was a boy; now he was a famous musician called The Jazz Man. The rolling pin had been discovered in the café when they remodeled it years ago. No one knew how old that was although the handle was engraved with a woman's name. The mirror had come out of the farmhouse where Linda and her sister, Lucy, had grown up.

"I'm keeping a couple of tables for you to the side," Linda finally said. She gestured to them. "I have my special kids' table set up for the boys. It's got bibs, crayons, that kind of thing. A special tablecloth they can color on."

Linda had her trademark white chef's apron on and a streak of gold in her dark hair. It had been a long time since Linda wore streaks, Conrad thought. When she first started with the café she used to have a different color in her hair every few days. But she'd calmed down in the years since then.

"We don't need anything fancy," Conrad muttered in case she was on some creative kick. "Place settings or food, just regular will do."

He remembered that the café owner

sometimes cooked gourmet romantic dinners for couples she decided should be together. He didn't want to scare Katrina away with peach flambé or anything. Besides, she had enough to deal with today. She'd have to talk to the sheriff some more after they ate.

As they walked, Linda touched Conrad on the elbow and motioned for him to hold back. They let Katrina and the boys go far enough ahead that they wouldn't be able to hear them.

"Why didn't you tell me your calendar woman was in town?" Linda whispered, low and urgent. She looked distressed. "I finally convince Tracy to come over for lunch, thinking the two of you could—you know—casually sit together. I thought it would cheer her up. And here you are—hours before lunch so there's no time for my pep talk to her. And there's no reason to give it anyway since you came in all lovey-dovey with some woman you picked off a calendar!"

"We're not lovey-dovey." He was aghast. They hadn't even kissed. "I was just wiping away the rain."

"People get wet in the rain. No one needs the drops wiped off their face."

"Well, maybe not, but—" He realized he had no reasonable excuse to offer so he let the sentence trail off. "I didn't pick her off the calendar. She just drove into town this morning. Muffler problems. She was going somewhere—I don't know where, but she didn't even mean to come here."

Linda shook her head in bewilderment. "What are the odds then? No one comes here who's been on a calendar anyone has seen."

"I know," Conrad admitted miserably.

"Especially not when we're praying for—well, you know."

"Believe me, I do."

Neither one of them said anything for a minute.

"Well," Linda said, her voice suddenly getting a bracing tone to it. "Since that's how it happened, my advice is to grab your chance. This calendar woman isn't going to wait around for you forever. Just because your uncle prayed her into town doesn't mean you can relax. You've got to show her a good time. Do more than talk about engines when you eat."

He was watching Katrina get her nephews settled at the kids' table. She put a bib on the youngest boy and handed both boys the crayons. They all seemed happy enough.

"Engines run the world," Conrad said when he looked back at Linda.

She rolled her eyes. "I'm not putting any napkins by your plate. All you do is draw those diagrams on them. I know Tracy wouldn't have minded, but this woman probably doesn't think like we do around here."

Conrad had to agree with that, but all he could say was, "I only diagrammed that forward thrust vector once. It got us to the moon."

"If you're going to talk about the moon, go outside and look at the moon."

"It's raining."

"You know what I mean." The café owner had lost her hesitation and seemed to be veering in the opposite direction. "It wouldn't hurt you to say a few nice things to the woman. She probably expects some oohing and ahhing. She's gorgeous. Men probably tell her that all the time. You better, too. And ask her what her favorite movie is. Make her think you have a life."

"I do have a life," Conrad said, but he

was talking to the air. Linda had already walked away.

Before he could gather himself together, Linda was standing at the table where he should be.

"Good, you found the bib and got everyone settled down," the café owner said to Katrina.

Conrad was almost afraid to join Katrina at the adult table with the pink plastic roses on it. But then he looked behind him and saw his aunt and uncle and Pete and Tracy all staring at him. He wouldn't want to make the explanations he'd need to make if he didn't sit down with Katrina and eat.

He smiled at the rear guard. Tracy's face looked pinched and she'd added some blonde to her brown hair and fussed it up some. Pete had on new boots.

"Just having a late breakfast," Conrad said with a forced smile. "Tracy, Pete, good to see you."

Both Tracy and Pete looked startled.

"We're not together." Pete's face reddened.

"I'm just here early for lunch," Tracy said at the same time. She took a step away from the ranch hand. "I was going to put another streak in Linda's hair before I eat, but—"

It was hard to know which way the wind blew there, Conrad thought. Ordinarily, Pete would be working at this time of day. He was dressed up in a clean snapped shirt and he had his dark hair slicked back though so it must mean something. Now that Pete was getting older, he'd make some woman a good husband, Conrad thought and then winced. People had probably been saying that same thing about him for years. Maybe Pete was just in town to buy some nails at the hardware store. A man could dress up without needing to walk down the aisle.

Conrad nodded to everyone and turned around to step closer to the table where his fate awaited him. Linda made her coffee strong and he was glad for it. He figured this breakfast would be a long, painful one. Linda might think he should take his chances, but he wasn't one to throw his heart out there where it was going to be trampled. There was nothing wrong with being cautious when it came to picking out a woman to date.

He sat down at the table and looked up to see Tracy still standing there. Now why couldn't he be sitting here with her? She wouldn't care if he rambled on about farm equipment or engines or the price of wheat. And, if she was going to trample on a man's heart, she wouldn't do it when she was wearing lethal high heels with those black straps that tied a man up like they did. Tracy could give him free haircuts, too. That had to count for something.

He picked up his menu. The thought came unbidden that he and Tracy had known each other for thirty years. Granted, she hadn't lived around here for all of that time, but she'd been back and forth. If they were meant to be together, wouldn't they have noticed it before now? He glanced back up at her. He wasn't even sure what kind of shoes she wore. He didn't think he'd ever noticed her feet.

Well, he told himself, no one ever said love came easy to a man. He'd just need to pay more attention. He could learn all he needed to know about Tracy's footwear. She would make him a fine wife if Pete wasn't going to make any moves—which, the more Conrad thought about it, the more he doubted. Pete was the most hard-core bachelor around. He might chase all the women, but he'd take care not to catch one.

Conrad wasn't like Pete. He wanted to

get married—someday. He was just being careful about it.

And Tracy might be the one for him. Granted, she didn't make his heart wobble, but he wouldn't wake up one morning like his father, either. He hadn't told his uncle, but there were days with his father that were so bleak Conrad didn't even want to be in the same house with him. He was probably seven years old at the time and he would spend days in the barn with the cats and the chickens, all of which would have starved if he hadn't taken over their feeding. Grief never left his father's house until the day the man died of a heart attack. Conrad had just turned sixteen, so he was old enough to stay on the ranch alone.

His uncle might think there was something wrong with him taking the safe road when it came to romance, but Conrad didn't agree. Conrad had seen where the other road could take a man, and he never wanted to go there. Loving someone might seem good at first, but it could lead to unimaginable tragedy. He'd rather be alone than go through what his father had.

Chapter Four

Katrina sipped on the hot lemon tea that Linda had put down in front of her.

"It's a soothing drink for a stressful day," the café owner said. "I sit down and have a cup myself on busy days."

"Oh, I'm fine," Katrina said with a quick glance at Conrad. He had become distant when they came into this café and she thought she knew why. His uncle, probably without thinking, must have told the people here that she was on the verge of being arrested. She didn't blame Conrad for wanting to be sure his friends knew he wasn't getting too familiar with someone like that.

"I'm just passing through town," she said, loudly enough for everyone to hear the words. Of course, technically the sheriff might have something to say about that, but she had to believe Leanne would answer the phone sometime today.

After Katrina's declaration, no one even looked back at her. Which was strange because they all seemed to have been looking at her before she spoke.

Linda excused herself and went to get the rest of their breakfast.

"Have you seen the new George Clooney movie?" Conrad asked.

"No, is there one?" Katrina's attention was on the boys sitting at the table across from them. Linda had just set down pancakes in front of them that had mouse ears and what looked like dried blueberries for eyes. Or maybe the eyes were—

"Do kids choke on raisins?" she looked up and asked Conrad. He'd be the kind of guy to know something like that. He probably knew how to do the Heimlich maneuver, too.

"I suppose they could." He looked startled. "It's not likely, though. Why?"

She nodded her head toward the pancakes. "Look at that. They could get those raisins stuck in their throats and hurt themselves with those plastic juice glasses.

I don't know how parents do it." She turned back and looked at him. "I've heard milk allergies can start around the boys' ages. Do you think they should be drinking it?"

"What are they going to eat?" Conrad asked, looking bewildered.

She glanced over at her nephews and noticed they were eating too fast. And they had white rings of milk around their mouths. If they were allergic to something, she didn't even know what to look for.

"I wonder if they have soy milk here." Katrina started to look around for someone to ask. Fortunately, Linda was coming out of the kitchen with a couple of platters, probably for their table.

Katrina hadn't been able to concentrate enough on the menu to actually pick something out, so she'd asked Conrad to order for her.

"That smells wonderful," she said.

"There's bacon," Conrad said. "I wouldn't have ordered it if I knew you were one of those soy kind of people. I don't think Linda carries any of the bacon made out of vegetables."

"Do they make such a thing?" Katrina asked. He had her attention now. She'd never seen a man so nervous. She finally understood. "Don't worry. I'm not going to make a mad dash for freedom while I'm eating my bacon or anything."

"Oh, I didn't think—" He started but clearly couldn't finish the sentence with a good conscience.

She felt the tears start in her eyes again. She blinked hard to make them go away. He was not really anyone to her. He was just fixing the muffler on her sister's car. She'd pay him and that would be the end of it. She wasn't good at relationships; she froze up when she should open up. She had a hard time telling people how she felt. But it was okay. There was no reason to care what he thought about her, anyway.

Linda set the two platters down on their table. "There you go. Two farm fresh breakfasts with fruit."

"Thank you," Katrina said as she looked up and forced herself to smile. She wasn't going to cry again today, especially not in front of this man.

"Conrad always orders the best breakfast around," Linda gushed as she moved the salt and pepper shakers into the middle of the table. "He knows how to—well, how to entertain a lady." Linda paused, looking stricken. "Not that he entertains many of them. I mean, not in that way—he usually comes in for dinner, not breakfast. I—"

"It's okay, Linda," Conrad said.

Katrina looked away. "I'm just passing through," she repeated. She blinked again. "I had a problem with the muffler on my sister's car and he's fixing it."

She glanced back up.

Linda nodded. "He's good at that, too." Then she looked down at Conrad. "He's actually good at many things. Why, I think he helped paint the mural on the side of that barn on the far edge of town. He's got a real talent."

"I operated the forklift and helped paint the clouds on the top," Conrad said dryly. "It wasn't much."

"Now, don't be modest," Linda said as she put her hands in the front pockets of her chef apron. "If either of you need anything else, you just let me know. That melon is sweet."

"It looks delicious," Katrina said. The plate in front of her had an egg, sunny side up, with two slices of bacon and a short stack of pancakes. The slices of melon were on the side.

"I'll bring the syrups right out. I have

maple and blueberry," Linda said as she turned to leave. "And I'll bring more pancakes for the boys, too."

"Could you make them without the eyes?" Conrad asked.

"Sure," Linda said. "I'll make dollar pancakes. You know, the plain round ones."

"Thanks," Conrad said.

Katrina blinked again.

"Don't cry," Conrad said softly after Linda had walked away.

"I'm not crying. I have—my face is just wet from the rain."

She still didn't look up at him.

"You don't have to eat anything you don't like," Conrad said. "I can order something else."

"Don't be ridiculous, this is perfect." Katrina lifted her fork and tried to smile even though she had no appetite now.

Conrad nodded. "You'll need your strength."

"You think I'm going to jail, don't you?" She sat back and looked at him.

He shook his head. "I just think it's going to be a long day. The sheriff hasn't come in to say he's reached anyone at the number you gave him. He's not likely to just say you can leave town. He might not look so tough, but Sheriff Wall is like a pit bull when he's on the job. He won't let go once he knows what he has to do."

"Well, you would know him better than I do," she said. And with that she used her fork to spear a piece of melon.

Conrad watched Katrina as she finished the last of her food. He looked over and saw that the boys were done, too.

"Let's get out of here." He put down three ten-dollar bills on the table. Linda would have a good tip. "I'll take you down to that sign you want to see and we'll see about getting you set up to take your picture."

"The lighting is not good enough to take the pictures now. I'll have to take them tomorrow if it's not cloudy. Come on, boys," she added as she looked over at them. "Let's get your coats back on."

Conrad noticed that her face was getting a little more color to it.

"You can at least see the sign, though," he said. "And I can stop on the way out and ask Tracy if she knows any young women that fit what you need. She cuts hair so she might know of some blondes."

"Is that the woman who's been looking at us?" Katrina asked as she pulled Zach's red coat over his arms. Ryan seemed to be managing his own.

Conrad wondered how she could tell who had been looking at them. He knew everyone was keeping an eye on their table.

"She likes you," Katrina said matter-of-factly as she stood and took her jacket off the back of her chair.

"Well, I always tip her when she cuts my hair." Conrad stood up.

Katrina looked at him skeptically and smiled softly. "I don't think it's your hair that is troubling her right now."

Conrad knew he shouldn't, but he turned around so he could look back and see what Katrina was talking about. He swiveled back. "She's not even looking at me."

"Not now," Katrina agreed as she put her jacket on. "But she was looking. I don't think she likes me very much."

"She doesn't even know you. Why would she—"

Katrina gave him a look that shot right through him. Then she nodded. "She's jealous all right."

Conrad was speechless. "No—"

Katrina shrugged. "Suit yourself then. But I recognize that stare."

She gathered up the boys and walked toward the door. Conrad followed behind them. He told himself it wasn't because he liked to watch Katrina walk. Although he did wonder how she swayed the way she did.

"We'll wait for you on the porch," she said when she opened the door.

Leave it to Katrina to cut out when he could use some moral support. It was up to him to ask the favor of Tracy.

"Good seeing you here," he greeted Tracy as heartily as he could. "Your hair's looking good."

"It's the same cut as always."

"I was hoping you might be able to help me out," he said. He couldn't stand to inch his way up on this.

"Oh?"

"My—" He stopped in a panic. He should have thought this through. "My customer," he continued. "She's trying to get a business started as a photographer and she wants to take a picture of a local couple looking at the heart sign down the road. She needs a young blonde woman, pretty and expressive, to be one of the models in the shot. It's supposed to be romantic and I thought you might know someone who—"

Tracy was silent.

Conrad forced himself not to fidget.

"Who's the man?" Tracy finally asked.

"What—" Conrad started. "What man?"

Tracy looked at him like he was slow. "The man that's going to be in the picture with this blonde you want me to find. Any woman's going to want to know who the man is if she's going to be taking some romantic picture with him."

"That makes sense. I didn't hear her mention the man. But I'll go ask."

Conrad fled the café. He wasn't cut out to be a negotiator.

"Well, what'd she say?" Katrina asked when he burst out of the café. She was standing quietly on the other side of the porch with the boys. The air was chilly and they all had their hands in their pockets.

"She wants to know who the man is that's going to be there with the blonde."

"I don't see why she needs to know that. It's not like they need to kiss or anything," Katrina said in exasperation. "If you watch the boys, I'll go talk to her."

"We'll all go," Conrad said as he gathered

the boys around. He needed to know what Tracy said, too.

The café was warm when he opened the door to step back inside. Katrina didn't stand still long enough to appreciate it, though. She went right over to Tracy.

"It doesn't matter who the man is. They'll be gazing into each other's eyes. That's all."

Tracy shrugged. "It still matters if the guy has a girlfriend. She won't want him gazing into any other girl's eyes. It could cause problems if you have the wrong man."

"I haven't asked any men yet," Katrina said. "Right or wrong."

"Pete could do it," Tracy offered.

Conrad heard a strangled sound behind him. Pete had just walked over.

"Me?" the ranch hand said. "In a picture?"

"A picture of romance," Conrad said just so he could see the color leave Pete's face.

"I imagine you've kissed your share of women," Tracy said a little tartly as she shot Pete a look that Conrad couldn't interpret. "It shouldn't be much of a problem to just gaze into their eyes soulfully."

"Well—I—" Pete stammered. "I have a job."

"It won't take long," Katrina said. "We can forgo the makeup and—"

"Makeup!" Pete exclaimed. "I'm not wearing any makeup. If word of that got out I'd lose my job."

"Nonsense," Katrina said. "No one could fire you for wearing makeup. It wouldn't be legal."

"Getting fired would be the least of my worries," the ranch hand said. "I wouldn't be able to show my face in the bunkhouse. I'd have to sleep out in the barn. I don't know where I'd eat. Why, I'd starve to death."

"Well, we won't do makeup," Katrina persisted. "So all you'd need to do would be to have your hair done."

"I just trimmed it. It's ready to go," Tracy said.

Conrad noticed his old friend was looking considerably more cheerful now that she could torment the ranch hand.

"Well, who's the woman going to be?" Pete demanded belligerently. He looked like he was going to continue with some choice words, but Katrina held up her hand.

"I don't think we know yet," she said. She glanced down at the boys standing beside her, looking on in wide-eyed amazement. "Remember we have children here."

The boys looked up, seeming even more curious.

"If you'd be doing it, I'd agree," Pete finally said with a sly look at Katrina. "I could throw in a kiss or two if you want."

Pete gave a wicked smile and the whole café was absolutely silent.

"He's going to kiss you?" Katrina's oldest nephew finally asked in awe. "Like on television?"

Conrad felt a kick to his gut that he didn't dare act on. He had no right to interfere with Katrina kissing anyone. He noticed Tracy had a sour look on her face, too. In all of the years he had known the hairstylist, Conrad had never known her to look wretched. Why, she almost looked like she was in love with Pete.

"Katrina can't do it," Conrad said with as much authority as he could muster. There was no point in tormenting Tracy. "I'm going to ask one of the married women."

"For romance?" Pete asked, his jaw dropping in astonishment.

"Getting married doesn't kill romance," Conrad continued. He sure hoped that was true. "At least with their husbands. They still know how to kiss. You should know that, Pete."

"Me? I've never kissed a married woman. Not that you have, either. What would you know about what marriage does or doesn't do to women?"

"Hearsay," Conrad said and then looked right at Pete. "Just come to town tomorrow morning early. Make it just after dawn. That'll give us plenty of time before Sunday school. You haven't been for a while and it'll do you good to go to church, too. We'll meet at the sign. There'll be nothing to it."

"Well, I don't know—"

"I'll fix that knocking sound in your pickup for free," Conrad said. "That old Ford truck is going to fall apart if you don't do something pretty soon."

"Well, if you put it that way," the ranch hand said and then grinned. "I'll be there ready to do some kissing."

"Gazing," Tracy interrupted. "She's only asking for the gazing in the eyes thing."

"I never do anything halfway," Pete said and winked at Katrina's nephews. "There's a lesson in that for you boys."

"Zach's only three," Katrina protested.

But the ranch hand was already putting his Stetson on his head and walking to the door.

Conrad turned to Tracy. "I'll see that there's no kissing."

Tracy smiled back at him a little sadly. All the spark had gone out of her face. "It doesn't matter. He's kissed hundreds of women anyway. What's one more?"

"Well, the woman we get may not want to kiss him anyway," Katrina said with some satisfaction. Then she stopped. "I forgot. I might not be here tomorrow. The sheriff will talk to Leanne and I'll leave."

"I wouldn't worry about that," Conrad said.

"But—"

"We'll talk about it on the way to the sign," Conrad said as he started to usher the boys out of the café. He didn't think it would help anyone to say that the sheriff wouldn't let her leave town unless he knew how she came to be in that old car.

They were almost to the door when Katrina whispered, "But what will we do if the sheriff doesn't let me go? What if Leanne and Walker don't answer their phone at all today? Maybe they're off on some romantic adventure."

"I don't think your sister and her husband would leave without telling you. Not when you have the boys," Conrad said, keeping his voice low. He looked down at Katrina's nephews. They were standing very still in that way children did when they were nervous.

As careful as he was, Conrad figured some of his words had escaped because he saw his aunt Edith walking toward them. She'd been Mrs. Hargrove until she married his uncle a year or so ago. No one had been able to get used to calling her Mrs. Nelson so she became Edith to everyone and Aunt Edith to him.

No matter her name, she was the heart of Dry Creek.

Right now, she was wearing an apron over one of her gingham print housedresses and had her hair pinned back in a careless bun. She had white orthopedic shoes on her feet and an old gray coat hanging from her shoulders. She looked like she was in a hurry to go somewhere. But, if there was a child in need anywhere in Dry Creek, she would be there even if she had to interrupt her baking to do so.

She smelled like spices when she got closer.

She smiled gently as she put her hands on the boys' shoulders and then bent down until she was at eye level with them. "You boys are welcome to stay at our house for a while. I'm going to be baking gingerbread cookies today. I've already got the dough stirred up and you can help me use the cookie cutters to make the men."

"Will they have eyes?" Ryan asked eagerly. "We like the eyes."

Aunt Edith looked up at Katrina. "You're welcome to come, too, dear. You won't want to spend your day just waiting over at Conrad's. Who knows how long it will take him to fix that muffler?"

"Oh—I—" Katrina stammered and then she looked at Conrad.

"Katrina might be busy. But the boys will need a place to take a nap later," he said.

"Only Zach takes a nap," Ryan protested. "I'm six."

"That's right. You're a big boy," Edith said as she straightened up and put her hands behind her back to ease some pain. She clearly didn't bend as easily as she used to.

"I appreciate you doing this, Mrs.—" Katrina started and then stopped.

"This is my aunt." Conrad started the introductions. "Katrina Britton, meet Mrs. Hargrove-Nelson. We call her Edith. She'll help you with the boys. "

"He's right," Edith said with a soft smile. "I'm home all day so just bring the boys by when you're ready. I have the oven going for the cookies so I'll be there."

Conrad could see Katrina relax. "Thank you."

"I could even take them with me now if you'd like. I have some toys they might like to play with."

"What kind of toys?" Ryan asked.

"There's no need for them to be out in the rain," Conrad said to Katrina. "They won't care about seeing that sign anyway."

Katrina nodded. "I guess if the boys want to go—"

The boys nodded and shyly gave Katrina a hug when she opened her arms to them. Then she patted them on their heads and let them go.

"There's no one in town better to keep an eye on them," Conrad said as they watched the boys walk away with his aunt and uncle.

"It does make sense," Katrina agreed, her voice low even though there was no one around them any longer. "I don't really want them there when I talk to the sheriff anyway."

"Yeah, well, let's go then," Conrad said.

He had been going to show her the sign first, but maybe they should just go ahead and see what the sheriff had to say. That way, when she saw the sign, she could devote her full attention to it.

"I hope you're not disappointed," he said as they walked back out on the café porch. "It's just a sign."

"I don't care what it looks like. I'm going to make it work," she said. "I have to."

Which only made him more nervous. He wished now that he'd given more than ten dollars to the cause when the teenagers in town had taken up a collection to place a bench by the sign. He suspected they only wanted it so they'd have someplace to sit and hold hands in summer. Well, he figured they couldn't get into very much trouble doing that since someone could come down the road at any time.

They had the bench on order, but no one had received it yet so there was nothing around the sign but mud and dried grass. And a few small boulders someone had hauled over for sitting. The last he heard no one had painted the signpost again, either. Every winter, it seemed to get a little more chipped. He liked the weathered look of the sign, but a photographer might not.

He wondered what it would take to get everyone to agree to put a new coat of paint on the signpost. It might be an odd attraction for a town, but the people here had taken that old metal post to their hearts and they were particular about anything that was done to it. If he understood love, he might understand about the post, he told himself. Right now, though, he felt clueless.

Chapter Five

After they stepped out of the café, Katrina took a minute to stand in the shelter of the porch. More dark clouds had moved in and cold rain was being blown around by the wind. She could see Edith and Charley Nelson walking with the boys down the street, all four of them with their heads down. Then she saw Charley stop and pick up Zach so he could ride on his shoulders. No one seemed to mind all the mud.

Her nephews would do fine with the older couple. Besides, it would only be for a couple of hours. By then, if all went well, she and the boys would be driving back to Leanne's place with nothing more than a good story to tell.

She patted the small pocket on the side

of her jacket. She missed having her cell phone with her. She hadn't been able to give a number to the Nelsons. Of course, they would both know to call the gas station if they had any problems with the boys. "Your aunt has your number. Right?"

Conrad looked over at her. "My phone number? Sure."

He was standing at the edge of the porch, waiting for her. When he left the gas station earlier, he'd put on a buffalo plaid jacket. She just now noticed he'd turned up the corduroy collar and it made him look like a lumberjack.

"You okay?" he asked. "It must be near freezing out here."

She nodded and put the collar up on her jacket. Unfortunately, the leather jacket only had a shallow band of a collar. If she was going to stay around here longer, she'd need to get a warmer jacket. Now, what made her think about that? She'd rather go back inside the café, but the sheriff was waiting.

She looked down the street. She was a good hundred yards from the station, but she could see that the sheriff's car was still parked right where it had been.

There were no sidewalks so she would

have to walk through mud to get to the asphalt. She really should have made sure her walking shoes were in the trunk of her sister's car. She had remembered to move her photography equipment, she should have thought of the shoes, too.

After a few steps, she felt the heels of her shoes suddenly go down.

"Oh." The sinking caught her off guard.

Her heels sank into the mud and were resting on the frozen ground beneath the slush.

"What's wrong?" Conrad stepped over and steadied her arm.

"I think I'm stuck," Katrina confessed. When he'd taken her arm, he'd also stepped closer. She hadn't quite realized how tall he was. Of course, she'd shrunk an inch when her heels slid down in the mud. And his shoulders were broad enough to block the rain so she was happy to stand there while he looked down at the ground.

Conrad frowned. "You're going to ruin those shoes."

"Well, I can't go barefoot."

"No, you can't," he agreed grimly. "Not in this. So hold on to your hat."

"I don't have a hat."

He didn't answer her. Instead, he scooped her up and settled her into his arms, her muddy shoes dangling off the ends of her equally muddy feet.

"Oh," she breathed.

His jacket was wet, but where it was open his shirt was dry. That's where he nestled her. "There. I'll get you to the asphalt at least."

"You don't need to—" Katrina started, but he was already walking with her. She hadn't realized he was quite so strong. She could feel the muscles of his arms through his jacket and she could see the underside of his chin. Being swept off her feet like this was really quite romantic. It made her think of her whole goal for the day. "Do you ever go without your shirt?"

"What?" He stopped so quick she thought he might drop her.

"I was thinking of the stop sign picture. If you had your shirt unbuttoned and—"

"No one is going to take a picture at that stop sign with their shirt hanging open. Not in this weather. Not me, not Pete. No one."

"Well, I just thought it would be romantic. You know, like those old movie stars. Tarzan and Jane."

"Tarzan!" Conrad set her down more

abruptly than necessary. "He didn't even own a shirt! And I don't think he ever saw a snowstorm."

Fortunately, they had reached the asphalt and her shoes didn't sink. She was standing very close to him though and it gave her a dizzy feeling in her stomach. He was looking down and his eyes were dancing with laughter.

"Well, other movie stars go bare-chested, too," she said just so she could watch his eyes. "Tom Cruise. George Clooney. You could be one of those."

He stared at her, speechless. Then he growled. "If you want movie star romance, here it is."

And, with that, he kissed her.

It was an impulse. She knew that right away, even without the chuckle in his throat. But then, when it should have ended, it didn't. Instead, his lips were coaxing hers to move with him. Suddenly, it wasn't just his lips; the temperature of the air around them warmed up so much she didn't even feel the cold on her face. Or on her feet, either. What had happened to her feet? She wondered if she was standing on the asphalt or if she had slipped back into the mud.

Maybe that would account for why she felt so off balance.

And then Conrad moved slightly. Instead of kissing her lips, he was rubbing his thumb along the line of her jaw. He had his head bent to hers and their foreheads were touching. His breath turned the air between them white.

"You're sweet," he murmured.

"Me?" she squeaked.

He nodded. "Maybe, if you stay around for a while, we could—"

And then she remembered. She swallowed. How could she have forgotten?

"I can't date you," she said in a whispered rush.

It was silent. Conrad finally pulled his forehead away.

"Well, I understand, of course," he said stiffly. "We don't even know each other. Besides—" He stopped, took a step away, and then spun around. "No, come to think of it, I don't understand. Are you worried about the sheriff taking you to jail? That will all be over once he talks to your sister."

"So you believe me about that?"

"Of course, I believe you. The boys know you're their aunt so I figure their mother must have told them you were. Those boys don't look worried about anything. Besides, I've looked under the hood and no one would steal that car you're driving. So I figure you must be worried about going to jail, but that's not going to happen."

Katrina shook her head. She was tempted to tell him everything about her health and her childhood. But, he was right, they didn't know each other very well. "There are worse things than spending a few days in jail."

"What do you mean?" His eyes were quiet now, searching hers.

"I can't tell you," she said.

"I see." Everything about him closed down. "Well, it's not a problem. I should be getting back to the station anyway."

And, with that, he turned and started walking back to his business, leaving Katrina standing in the middle of the asphalt road. The rain was still coming down and she realized she had forgotten the umbrella back at the café. She didn't mind the cold wet of the day, though. It would hide any tears that came and she had no use for sunshine anyway.

She wished it had been different, but she knew she'd done the right thing. She liked

Conrad, but she was a little bit of a loner at the best of times. She didn't make casual friends. She didn't trust easily. It wasn't fair to ask anyone to walk beside her until she knew more about the cancer. Her old boyfriend had certainly agreed with that. Maybe after she saw the doctor again, she could come back here and set things right.

Conrad couldn't believe what he'd done. It might sting that Katrina didn't want to go out with him, but he should be more gracious than that. He was a grown man, not a little kid. His only excuse was that his uncle's prayer request had churned up expectations in him that he shouldn't be thinking about.

"Conrad!" He heard the shout and looked up.

Sheriff Wall was jogging toward him with a scowl on his face and a hand on his head to keep his hat from blowing off. Half-frozen rain was coming at both of them and, outside of his name, Conrad couldn't hear anything else the lawman was saying. Then the sheriff pointed at something behind him.

Conrad turned around. Ah, yes, the sheriff was worried about Katrina escaping.

"I'm sorry," Conrad said, as the lawman got closer. "She'll be here in a minute."

Sure enough, Katrina was walking down the asphalt road with more dignity than he possessed. Her long black hair was flying. A lesser woman would be bowed by the wind, but not her. She had taken off her high heels and was walking barefoot in the rain.

Conrad turned back to see the sheriff looking at him.

"What's wrong with you?" the lawman demanded. "You don't know who this woman is. She could be anyone. And you're out in the middle of the street kissing her like you're a couple of teenagers."

"She doesn't want to have anything to do with me," Conrad confessed miserably.

"Well—" the sheriff said gruffly and then cleared his throat.

"I more or less asked her out and she said no," Conrad continued just in case the man didn't get the full picture.

"At least one of you has some sense then," the sheriff finally said. His voice did have some reluctant sympathy, though. "I heard about that prayer request of yours. My wife has it stuck to our refrigerator door with a magnet."

Conrad grimaced. "That was my uncle's doings."

"Yeah, well," the sheriff said and then gave him a short pat on the back. "I think you should pick a woman who isn't in the middle of a theft investigation—or worse."

Conrad felt icy cold. "What do you mean worse?"

The sheriff nodded grimly. "Here she comes. I'll tell you both when we get back inside. No sense in us catching pneumonia out here talking."

No one had said much when Katrina came up to the two men. The wind was miserable by then and everyone had their heads down. The sheriff pointed to the gas station and they all started walking against the wind to get there.

Katrina was exhausted. After a few steps, Conrad put his arm around her and helped her along. She didn't really need his help, but his shoulders provided some shelter for her and she wasn't about to refuse his kindness.

The sheriff was the first one to step inside the gas station office.

"Your aunt and uncle have the boys?" he turned to ask Conrad. Rain was still running down the man's face, but he had a serious look to him and he didn't even wipe the drops away.

Conrad nodded. "We thought it would be best."

"They have toys," Katrina added.

"They'll be well taken care of," the lawman said and then he stood there.

"Have you heard from Leanne or Walker?" Katrina asked, beginning to worry. It was clear something had changed since the sheriff had talked to her earlier, but she couldn't imagine what it could be. "They called back, didn't they?"

"No," the sheriff said. "But I had one of the men from the tribal police go over and check their house. I thought maybe they were just outside or something."

"Leanne doesn't spend much time outside. It's too early for her garden."

"Yeah, well, she wasn't there," the sheriff said. "Walker wasn't there, either."

Katrina swallowed. Maybe that was good news. "They've been having problems. They could have gone away for the day and—"

"Someone broke into the house," the lawman continued. He kept looking at Katrina like he was judging her response.

"A window was smashed and everything was messed up inside."

"They didn't have a fight, did they?" Katrina asked. She'd worried about Leanne marrying Walker, but she'd never thought of physical violence. She'd known he intended to live on the reservation and she didn't think her sister would do well there.

"The man said it didn't look like a fight. The furniture wasn't broken. Mostly drawers were upended and the clothes in the closets were thrown on the bed. No real damage done though. Usually, in a fight, a lamp gets broken or something."

"Could they have been packing?" Conrad asked.

The sheriff shook his head. "Everyone's things were gone through. The boys. The wife. The husband. It was more like a search, but that's not all."

Katrina couldn't stand it any longer. "What is it?"

She felt her breath catch in her throat again.

The sheriff was looking at her, his eyes blank of any emotion. "There were traces of blood on the doorjamb. Someone could have cut themselves breaking into the house. Or someone could have grabbed the jamb on their way out of the house if they were injured."

"No," Katrina groaned.

"Do you mind if I look at your hands?" the sheriff asked.

"What?" Katrina asked.

"Your hands," the man repeated.

Numbly, she held them up.

"To the elbow, please," the sheriff asked and she took her jacket off.

Conrad held out his hands and she gave the garment to him. His dark eyes followed her movements and she couldn't figure out what he thought. The light was low in the office and not much more was coming through the windows. It was raining steady outside. The faint smell of coffee hung in the air.

Katrina pushed up the sleeves on the ivory pullover she was wearing. Then she spread her fingers wide and let the sheriff take a good long look. Then she turned them over.

"I'd never hurt my sister," she whispered when he finally finished examining her. "She's my only family."

The sheriff wasn't moved by her words. "An awful lot of violence happens in families. And you said yourself the two of you had your problems. You mentioned you haven't been in close contact for a long time."

"Yes, but—" Katrina looked over at Conrad. "Truly, I wouldn't."

He nodded and turned to the sheriff. "If you want to ask more questions, I think we should wait until we can get a lawyer here."

"A lawyer!" Katrina protested. "I don't need a lawyer."

The sheriff turned toward the window. "There's a forensics team on the way to the house now. They're going to try to get a handle on the bloodstain. If it doesn't match either of the two adults living in the house and it doesn't match yours, we might be able to eliminate you from consideration. The tribal council has samples of their blood and will confirm or deny for us."

"I have nothing to hide," Katrina said. "You're welcome to take a blood sample from me."

The sheriff nodded. "I'll do that. I have a kit in the car. I'm inclined to believe you for now, though. Mostly because of the boys. They gave me a pretty thorough accounting of when you left this morning. They didn't mention you going back to the house afterward and boys like that would notice a broken window."

"But what's going to happen?" Katrina asked. "You need to be looking for Leanne. She wouldn't have just disappeared. The boys and I were supposed to be home by five o'clock. She was making chicken for dinner. I saw her take it out of the freezer."

"We're already looking for her," the sheriff said.

"You and the boys will stay with me at my uncle's house," Conrad said as he stepped forward. "Just as long as you need to until this works out."

"Like I said, we'll know more soon, I'm sure. It helps that we know where your sister's car is," the sheriff said.

Katrina looked at the lawman. "She must have taken my car. A beige Lexus with a moon roof. I got the model with extra horsepower. Maybe if she's in the car, she's running for help."

The sheriff took a notepad out of his pocket. "There were no vehicles at the site. Give me the description and I will pass it along to highway patrol."

Katrina nodded. She began with the license plate number and finished up with the decal she had in the window saying she was a member of the Huntington Rose Society. She'd joined before she got cancer and never had planted the rose bush she'd meant to.

"Leanne knew we were coming down I-90 this way. Maybe if we put something out on the road she'd know to take this exit if she drove by looking for us."

"I have an old piece of plywood. I can put a sign out with the boys' first names on it," Conrad offered.

"Sounds good," the sheriff said as he finished with his notes. There was nothing more to say.

"Why don't I take you over to my uncle's house," Conrad said, then looked at the sheriff.

The lawman nodded. "Just be sure—" He stopped to sigh. "Well, you know the drill."

"Yeah," Conrad said as he took her arm again.

Katrina was content to be led. If her sister was in danger, she felt as though she should be doing something, but what could she do? She and her sister had seen their share of tragedy as children and she'd never been sure if that drew them closer together or pushed them further apart. Whichever it had done, it had intensified their relationship. What pained her sister, hurt Katrina. That's part of the reason she hadn't been able to be too close when her sister married Walker. She didn't want to feel the distress she knew was coming when Leanne became unhappy living on the reservation.

The cold rain hit Katrina in the face when she left the sheltered area around the gas station pumps. She moved closer to Conrad's warmth. Her sister accused her of shying away from strong emotions. She willingly admitted it. Her emotions were too messy. She had to stay away from them—it's what kept her in balance.

"You forgot your Closed sign," she murmured to Conrad as he put an arm around her shoulder. "People won't know you're not here."

"Shh, it's okay," Conrad said. They came to the end of the concrete and he moved his arm away from her. She didn't have time to miss it, though, because then he lifted her effortlessly as he had done before and settled her against his chest. He carried her through the rain to a white picket fence. The gate opened easily and he walked up to a plain two-story house with dormant rose bushes on each side of the front porch. They reminded her of the Huntington roses she hadn't planted.

And then she suddenly realized the condition she was in. "I can't go to your aunt's. I don't have any shoes on—no clean ones anyway."

Conrad gave a soft laugh. "My aunt Edith is perfectly able to cope with missing shoes."

"But the sheriff—"

"She can cope with that, too."

He knocked on the door and moments later Edith opened it with a smile. Warm air and the smell of ginger welcomed them inside.

"It feels like home," Katrina said with a sigh. She felt hope for the first time in hours. Maybe things would turn out all right. If only the sheriff could find her sister. And Conrad would continue being nice to her. And Edith turned out to be everything her smile promised.

Chapter Six

It was four o'clock before the sheriff came to the door. By that time, Katrina had stood at the kitchen counter in hand-knitted slippers and squeezed out scrolls of yellow frosting hair on thirty-seven gingerbread men who were lined up on a white dish towel. Once Edith found out she was from Los Angeles, the older woman suggested they make their cookies into beach surfer men. Katrina had to admit they were cute. Edith had even made gingerbread surfboards for them to carry and the two women had giggled together as they frosted them in beach colors.

The ring of the doorbell changed all that, though. Edith dried her hands on her apron to go answer the door, but then they could both hear the door open without her. Conrad had been working, but he apparently closed his gas station early because he was walking in with the sheriff. The voices of both men could be heard as they came through the living room.

Katrina felt her stomach knot up. "I suppose they've heard something about that blood."

"You'll be fine." Edith reached out to hold Katrina's hand. "I know you told the sheriff everything you knew, but it's not too late to say you want to have a lawyer with you."

Katrina squeezed the older woman's hand. Sitting in this kitchen had made Katrina miss her mother. She'd been twelve when both her parents died. Before that, they had always been too busy with church work to spend much time with anything domestic. She'd never made gingerbread men or sat and discussed what kind of curtains someone should make for their dining room. Maybe, she thought to herself, she was really missing the mother she'd always wanted to have.

"I'm fine without a lawyer," Katrina said and then added shyly, "But I'd like you to sit with me."

Edith's eyes brightened and she blinked. "Of course, dear."

Then she took off her apron. "We'll go sit in the dining room."

There were no curtains on the windows, but the shades were drawn so it was darker than the other rooms. Edith switched on an overhead light and the room was filled with a warm glow. A large mahogany table sat in the middle of the room with six matching chairs arranged around it. A natural lace runner ran the length of the table and a vase stood in the middle with blue plastic flowers. Along the left wall, there was a glass-topped buffet and on the right a large photo of a young blonde girl Edith had said earlier was her daughter, Doris, taken some forty years ago.

Edith had no sooner turned on the light than the sheriff and Conrad came through the archway leading from the living room. The sheriff took off his Stetson and Conrad started taking off his jacket.

The lawman looked serious so Katrina figured this was not a good report.

"Please, have a seat," Edith said to everyone.

The sheriff sat on one side of the table and Katrina was pleased that Conrad sat on the side with her and Edith. He sat to her left; Edith to her right. Katrina took a deep breath. Her nephews were upstairs watching a cartoon video with Charley so she didn't need to worry about them. She was not surprised when Edith reached out and took a hand, but then when Conrad took her other hand she almost burst into tears.

The lawman took her cell phone out of his pocket and handed it back to her.

He didn't say anything, though.

Everyone was silent for a few moments.

"Do you mind if we pray first?" Edith asked the sheriff and then looked at Katrina with a worried face. "I won't if you'd rather not, but—"

"No, it's fine," Katrina mumbled. She didn't think it would make any difference, but if it made Edith feel as if she was doing everything she could, Katrina would not stop her. She barely got her eyes closed before the older woman began.

"Our Father," Edith said with so much intimate warmth in her voice Katrina almost opened her eyes to see if someone had entered the small room. "We need Your help for our beloved Katrina and her sister and brother-in-law. We pray for Your protection to surround them, Father, wherever they are today. Give the sheriff and his colleagues what they need to know to unravel the troubles at the Rain Tree household. Be with us all as only You can be. In the name of Jesus, Our Precious Lord and Savior, amen."

No one said anything as they opened their eyes and settled back into where they were.

Finally, the sheriff cleared his throat. "They ran the tests on the blood from the doorjamb. It's not yours." He looked at Katrina. "And it doesn't seem to match either Leanne's or Walker's, either."

Katrina took a deep breath. "So I'm cleared?"

"Let's just say you are continuing to be less of a person of interest in the case—if there is a case," the sheriff said with a small smile. "We're not any closer to figuring out what happened, though."

"There haven't been any reports on my car?" Katrina asked. "I have a feeling if we find the car we will find Leanne."

"I put up that sign we talked about," Conrad said. "Right by the Dry Creek exit. But no one strange has driven into town."

"And it takes time to locate a car using an all-points bulletin," the sheriff said.

"Not around here it doesn't," Katrina muttered. "When I drove Leanne's car into Dry Creek, these people were all over it. It can't have been reported stolen for more than a few hours at that time."

"Well, not every town has a neighborhood watch like those men at the hardware store," the sheriff said with a quick grin before turning serious again. "I wish they did. In the meantime, I'm wondering if you'd let me look in Leanne's car. Maybe there's a clue there. Even something as simple as a gas receipt might help."

Katrina nodded. "Of course. The keys are at Conrad's station where he keeps the keys of the cars he's working on. There's a yellow disc at the top of the key chain that advertises some hotel."

"Maybe—" the sheriff began.

But Katrina was already shaking her head. "That hotel is in Texas and the key chain is old. Leanne would have told me if she was going that far away. There's really nothing else in the car except for Zach's car seat."

The sheriff shrugged. "Well, it was worth a try."

Conrad cleared his throat. "I'll look in the glove compartment when I go over to the station. Sometimes people keep old receipts there. Is the department treating this as a missing person's case then?"

"Yes, but the problem is that we can only suggest actions to the tribal authorities and, so far, all we have is a breaking and entering with a possible stolen vehicle. They're busy with other things, they say."

"They need to make it a priority." Edith had a small frown on her wrinkled face. "We'll need to add this to our church prayer bulletin if that's okay."

"My sister would like that," Katrina said. Leanne had handled their parents' deaths differently than she had. She might even still believe in prayer, even if she hadn't gone to church for some time.

Katrina faced the sheriff. "You'll let me know if you find anything about Leanne. Good or bad, I want to know."

"I'll tell you what I can," the lawman said. "If you had any idea of where she might go, it would be helpful for us to know."

"I wish I knew."

The sheriff nodded and rose up from the chair. "I better check back with the tribal police." He looked at her again. "Try not to worry."

Katrina waited for the lawman to leave the room and Conrad and his aunt waited with her. Finally, they heard the sound of the door closing.

"I need to go see my sister's house," Katrina said. "Maybe there's something I will notice that the police haven't."

Conrad squeezed her hand and she realized he still held it.

"I understand how you feel, but you have your nephews to think of. You're their only tie to their mother. They'll need someone to be here to comfort them if—" Conrad stopped.

Katrina gasped. "It wouldn't make any difference. There could be a hundred people here and if something has happened to their parents, it wouldn't make the slightest bit of difference."

"Oh, dear," Edith said as she put her hand over the one Katrina had lying on the table. "Did something happen to your parents when you were a child?"

She was going to say she couldn't talk about it, but then she looked at Conrad. She couldn't just keep saying everything was too private. And the truth was, she wouldn't mind if these two new friends knew. She wasn't quite sure why that was, but she didn't have time to question it.

"I was twelve," she began. She didn't want to look at anyone so she stared across the table at the picture of the girl, Doris. "Maybe about her age. My sister was about five years younger. Our parents were Christians, always busy in the church. Then one year they decided they were going to go for six months to work on a mission project in Africa. They were excited, showing us pictures of the babies and the families they were going to help. They'd never done anything like that before. They said they were going to help save the souls of those people. Leanne and I were going to stay with our aunt Bertha while they were gone. She smelled like cats. She had lots of cats."

Katrina felt hoarse, as if her throat was clogged with unshed tears even though it was completely dry. "Anyway, my parents went and there was a plane crash and they died in a country we couldn't even find on Aunt Bertha's maps. We looked and looked, but no one knew where it was."

"We didn't know what to do. Aunt Bertha

kept telling us that we should be happy our parents had been doing God's will when they died."

She didn't have the courage to ask the question when she was twelve, but it had burned in her ever since. "How could that be? Didn't God care about Leanne and me?"

"Oh, you poor dear," Edith murmured as she put her hand on Katrina's arm. "He cares very much about you. It was an accident."

"If He cared, He would have stopped it."

Everything was silent and then Conrad moved his chair close and pulled Katrina to him in a hug. "I know how that feels."

"It's all right. You don't have to say that."

"No," he said softly. "I *know* how that feels. My mother died when I was five and my father might as well have. I felt abandoned, too."

Katrina took a deep breath. It felt good to have told someone who understood. She looked to the other side of her and saw that Edith had gone back into the kitchen, leaving her alone with Conrad. She settled back into his arms.

They just sat there for the longest time.

Then Conrad felt the rubber band inside him loosen. "I never did want to talk about my parents, either. I don't think I even understood what I was feeling. I was so young."

Katrina nodded. "It was worse for Leanne. All we had for family was Aunt Bertha and she didn't really want us. When we were first staying there, after our parents had just left, she kept saying she couldn't wait for them to come back. Leanne started crying a lot, but when we heard about our parents she stopped. Maybe she knew no one was going to come rescue us then. We were stuck with Aunt Bertha and she was stuck with us. It was awful."

Conrad started to rub Katrina's neck. He could feel the tension in her. "I suppose that's why you never go into churches?"

She nodded. "I vowed I'd never set foot in a church again. How could God care so much about those people in Africa and not me and Leanne? We were right in front of His face in that church." She smiled slightly and looked up at him. "Back then my geography wasn't so good. I somehow thought if God was looking down on us in Ohio, He couldn't even see the people in Africa. And the other way around, too."

"I suppose we all think that when we're kids. Everything seems so far away."

"Leanne ended up on the Crow Indian reservation because she'd found some short-term mission project just like our parents had done. Fortunately, she didn't have to fly anywhere or I'd have tried to stop her. But the reservation was close and I thought she might find some peace in what she was doing. Instead, she met Walker and—" She looked up at him again. "I was just so mad that she was letting that project change her life that I said some awful things about her and Walker and the reservation where they were going to live."

"I'm sure she'll forgive you if you say you're sorry," Conrad said.

Katrina laughed. "You don't know Leanne. She'll want drama."

"Well, we'll give it to her then," Conrad said and then caught himself. "I mean, you'll give it to her."

Katrina was silent for a moment and then she said, "I hope we find her so I can."

Suddenly, there was a clatter of noise and the two boys burst into the dining room. Charley trailed behind them.

"We ran out of cookies," Ryan said as he held up a plate with some crumbs on it.

"How many cookies have you had?" Katrina said as she stood and walked over to them.

When she got to the boys, she forgot about cookies. She knelt down and looked each of them in the eye. "I want you both to know I care about you. We haven't had much time together, but if anything ever happened I would love you and keep you and—"

"Give us more cookies?" Zach asked hopefully.

Katrina gave a choked laugh. "Well, no, I wouldn't give you more cookies. But that's only because it's for your own good not to have them."

"Awhhh," Ryan said.

"Don't worry," Zach whispered loudly to his brother. "Mrs. Edith will give us some."

"You won't want to be too full to eat one of my aunt's dinners. They're even better than cookies," Conrad said.

The boys looked at him in disbelief.

"Besides, I think I remember where there are Lincoln Logs upstairs that can make a mountain."

"Can we crash the mountain?" Ryan asked.

"If you help build it," Conrad said, taking the boys away to show them the logs.

A half hour later, Conrad walked into his aunt's kitchen. She was washing dishes and Katrina was at the counter slicing carrots.

"I was wondering," he said to his aunt as he walked over to the sink and picked up a dish towel. "Did you keep those tables I had? You know the ones—"

His aunt looked up and nodded. "I don't know why you kept those things, but Charley put them in the desk in the spare room."

Conrad took a plate from the dish drainer and began to dry it. "I spent the whole summer on those tables when I was ten." He looked over at Katrina who glanced up from the carrots. "They were actuary tables and showed how likely people were to die at various ages."

"Oh," Katrina said in surprise as she put down her knife.

Conrad nodded. "I know. It wasn't very emotionally healthy. You might have been mad at God, but I spent all my time worrying. And it wasn't just about my father. I thought the mailman might be dying if he had a little cough. I wondered if my uncle was going to be able to come the next weekend. I had a lot to work through, let me tell you."

"I'm sorry," Katrina said softly. "I had no idea it was so hard for you."

Conrad swallowed. " I just wanted you to know."

He'd never told anyone about those tables except his uncle Charley. "I missed my mother more than I would have thought possible. She's what made our house a home. My father and I, we didn't know what to do without her."

Conrad set the dried plate down on the counter and looked at Katrina. "I imagine you felt the same way when your parents died so unexpectedly."

He saw the emotion grow in Katrina's eyes.

"I've never told anyone before how bad it felt," Katrina finally said. "It was a long time before I cared about anything or anyone after they died."

Katrina looked away from him and started cutting carrots again. He understood she needed some quiet. He turned back to the dishes.

After a few minutes, his aunt spoke.

"Conrad, I was hoping you might spend

the night here. We have the sofa even if the boys are in your room. They're predicting thunderstorms and everything just seems so unsettled," Edith said.

He nodded. "I was planning on it. I'll need to go back and get my toothbrush, though."

Until recently when he'd bought the old Gossett place and started fixing it up, he'd been staying with his aunt and uncle.

"Keep dry," Katrina said quietly.

He nodded. The truth was he wouldn't mind going out in the cold and wet. He wasn't used to telling someone about his mother's death and he still felt raw inside. For him, storms were sometimes more comforting than a sunny day. At least he knew the bad weather was already here so he didn't need to wonder when it was coming.

"Bring some clothes for church tomorrow," his aunt called out as he walked toward the door.

He nodded.

"I'll need to get my camera, too," Katrina said. "To take pictures of the heart sign."

"We can get that tomorrow," he said as he turned the handle on the door and then stood there. "I usually stop by the station on my way to church anyway so I'll just go early. I don't open up, but it's habit. I like to check anyway."

"You're careful about everything," Katrina said.

"I suppose so." He opened the door and stepped out quickly so the cold would not come in the house. He looked up and saw that the sky was deep gray in the east. They probably were in for some thunderstorms.

He put his jacket collar up for the walk back to the station. He wished he had more comfort to offer Katrina. All he could do was pray, though. He was glad that no one had ever told him that his mother's death had anything to do with the will of God. He didn't have any good answers for Katrina on that, but he knew God never intended for her and her sister to feel as though they'd been abandoned.

He opened the door to his gas station before he realized the reason he was so intent on making a home here in Dry Creek was because he'd never had one with his father after his mother died. Fixing up that old house was taking a lot of energy, but he felt hopeful with each nail he hammered. He wasn't just remodeling a house; he was re-modeling himself. Someday soon, he'd be a new man and his house would be a true home.

Chapter Seven

Katrina woke up with a start. She didn't know what had awakened her. The curtains on the bedroom were closed, but it was dark outside anyway. There was no rain or traffic noise. She lay stiff in the bed until she remembered she was in Edith's home. Then her cell phone rang. It must have rung earlier.

She thought it might be from the sheriff so she quickly flipped on the night-light and stood up. Edith had given her a cotton flannel nightgown to wear and she was grateful for it because of the temperature. The wood floor was chilly on her bare feet, but she didn't hesitate to walk over to the dresser where she'd put her purse last night.

She pulled the cell phone from her purse.

She saw it was five o'clock in the morning. Then she pressed the talk button. "Hello."

There was a moment's hesitation and then a whispered voice asked, "Katrina? Is that you?"

"Leanne!" Katrina was wide awake now. "Where are you?"

"I can't talk loud," her sister continued in a low voice. "I don't want anyone to hear me. I stopped to get gas and I opened your glove compartment and found your business card. I would have called earlier, but I—"

Leanne paused and Katrina could hear the sound of men's voices.

"Are you all right?" Katrina asked.

"Yeah, they were just a couple of truckers," her sister finally answered. "I'm somewhere along the I-90 freeway heading east. At a pay phone by the restroom."

"Get off at the Dry Creek exit," Katrina said. "I put a sign up with the boys' names on it so you'd see it."

"Oh, no," Leanne hissed. "You've got to take it down. I need to find you before Walker—"

The men's voices came closer again.

"Are you all right?" Katrina asked. "Did Walker threaten you?"

The voices receded.

"He just got really mad when I told him I'd lent you the car," Leanne said. "I've never seen him like that. He punched a hole in the wall and almost hit me. Then he said I needed to leave or I could be hurt bad. I was scared. That car is so old it's not worth anything. I took off in your car. He tried to follow me. I think he thought I was going to meet you, but I didn't know where you were."

"Is Walker still following you?" Katrina asked.

"I don't think so. I lost him when he had to stop and get gas in his pickup. Then I pulled off and rested for a while behind a warehouse. I figured if he cooled off some maybe—"

Katrina heard a door slam in the distance.

"Look, I've got to go," Leanne said. "Kiss the boys for me and I'll be there in a few hours."

Katrina looked at the clock again. "We'll probably be at the church."

"You?" Leanne said in astonishment and then the men's voices came closer and she hung up.

Katrina pressed the cold phone to her cheek as she listened to the dial tone. She was so glad her sister had finally called. Maybe she did owe someone her gratitude.

"Thank You—" she whispered. She looked up and then she swallowed. "Thank You, God. Whoever's up there on duty. Thank You for keeping my sister safe."

Well, that felt strange, she thought. She wasn't ready to do any forgiving, but she was grateful that Leanne was safe thus far. If God had something to do with that, she'd acknowledge it. That was only fair. Now that her sister knew to come to Dry Creek, she'd probably be here before church was over this morning. Maybe even before it began.

Katrina walked over to the window and pulled back the curtains. It was dark outside. There was an edging of frost around the window, but she could see Conrad's gas station from here. He had lights over the gas pumps and they lit everything up enough that she could see the whole building. The windows of the garage showed nothing but black inside, though. She wished Conrad had parked Leanne's car outside, but he clearly hadn't. He had brought the key to the car back with him last night and laid it on the dining room table.

The one thing she could do for Leanne

right now was to go take that sign off the freeway. She'd need a car to do that. And she'd have to get dressed.

Suddenly, the thought struck her that Conrad might not lock his building at night. It would be foolish not to, she knew that. But Edith had made the remark earlier today that most people didn't lock their doors around here. At least, the older woman had added, not unless there was a rodeo in Miles City.

Apparently, the rodeo was a big thing around here. Cowboys would come from all over and townspeople took extra precautions. She'd also heard that a woman, Lizette Bowman, came in from the ranch she shared with her husband, Judd, and opened her small bakery. She'd make enough of her legendary doughnuts to keep the rodeo men and everyone else happy for a few days.

Leanne could love this little town, Katrina told herself as she sat down to put on her jeans. If Walker was threatening her, maybe Leanne would keep herself and the boys away from him. Maybe they could come to Dry Creek and make a home here.

It was a fantasy, Katrina knew that.

Moving to Dry Creek was what she would like to do if she could. The buildings around here might be a bit weathered and wind-blown, but the people were rock solid. She'd made the mistake before of thinking that her sister would feel the same way she did; she didn't want to make that assumption again, even though she believed that if her sister got to know people like Edith and Conrad, she would be drawn to them. Of course, life was never that simple. Even for her, half of her was drawn to Dry Creek and the other half wanted to run away.

Katrina finished putting on the same ivory top she'd worn yesterday. Edith had lent her a comb and she tried to straighten out her hair. She'd also given her a tooth-brush and Katrina planned to stop at the bathroom and brush her teeth and get herself ready to go outside.

Conrad had a blanket wrapped around himself and he was lying on the sofa. He'd gone to bed in the clothes he'd worn all day long. He didn't have any nightwear with him and he liked the weight of his clothes, especially when the weather was cold like this. Besides, he wasn't totally at ease. The wind had blown some earlier and the fate of Katrina's sister kept twisting around in his mind. That's why he wasn't fully asleep when he heard the footstep overhead. It sounded like it was coming from the bedroom Katrina was using and, at first, he thought she had simply gotten up in the night to use the bathroom.

But then he heard footsteps coming down the stairs. Even that wouldn't have caused him to stir as she might have gotten thirsty and wanted a drink of water from the kitchen. But he could tell from the clicks that she was wearing her high heels. Now, why would she wear heels to the kitchen when his aunt had given her those cozy slippers?

Plus, given the way she was tiptoeing around in those heels, it seemed she didn't want to wake him up. That couldn't be good if she was going somewhere without telling anyone. She was still under suspicion, at least a little.

There were no lights in the living room and it was dark outside. His aunt had left a small light on by the dining room table, though, so it outlined the furniture around Conrad. He shifted slightly on the sofa so he could see the stairs better. He knew

Katrina couldn't see him, but he saw everything as she crept down the stairs. He noticed that she had her jacket on. Even her hair was combed. He hoped that maybe she was just so excited about that heart sign that she was going to sneak out and look at it again. It would be another hour or so before anyone else would be there, though.

Katrina didn't head for the front door. Instead, she walked right into the dining room and picked up the keys for her sister's car. He had left them on the table after searching the glove compartment of the car.

He stood up and Katrina squeaked in alarm.

"Going somewhere?" he asked. The blanket had fallen off him and he took a step closer.

"I thought you were asleep," she said as though he were the one in the wrong. "You scared me."

"Maybe," he noted. "I see you're going out."

"I was just going to see if your garage was unlocked," she started to sputter. "I—"

"You *what?*" It had never occurred to him that she would break into his garage. "I don't even keep any money over there."

She closed her eyes. He didn't know how he could tell because he could barely see her face. But it was evident in the sudden hunching of her shoulders and the way she looked like she might take flight. "I'm not stealing anything. I just need to go move the sign we put up. Leanne is worried about it being there."

"You talked to your sister?" Conrad asked. If he thought about it, he knew she wouldn't steal.

"She saw my cell phone number on one of my new business cards—the ones for my photography business." Her words were coming out breathless like she was frightened. He took a step closer to reassure her and was relieved that she didn't move back from him.

"It's okay," he said. "Take your time and—"

"Breathe," she added with a quick smile at him. "I know."

She took a deep breath and continued. "Leanne took my car and ran away from the house. She said Walker was angry that she'd lent their car to me and she was frightened. I didn't mean to cause them any trouble. I wonder if he's threatened her in the past."

"Did she say where she was?" Conrad asked.

"She was calling from a pay phone at some truck stop along the freeway. I told her where we were, but she said we need to take the sign with the boys' names down so Walker doesn't see it."

"Then that's what we'll do," Conrad said. "Just let me get my coat and we'll drive out to the freeway and pick up the sign. Why don't you write a note for my aunt so she'll know where we are if she gets up early to fix breakfast. Usually, she doesn't do that but she might want to make waffles since the boys are here."

Katrina nodded.

"I think we can wait until it's light out to call Sheriff Wall. He'll be glad you heard from your sister. I suspect Walker might be back on the reservation by now anyway. The tribal officials will have to handle him if he is."

It only took a few minutes for them to be ready to leave. Then Conrad took her hand and they walked out to get his car. The night was dark and there wasn't even a moon to light their way, but they went arm in arm through the silent town.

"We're here," Conrad said as they came to his house and walked up his driveway. "I'm in the process of remodeling everything so—"

"It's you," Katrina stopped. She was looking over at his yard. "You're the one with the garden gnome."

Conrad nodded. "It's a bit silly, I know. My uncle gave it to me as a housewarming present when I bought this fixer-upper. There's a store in Miles City that sells them."

"You need another one," Katrina said.

He looked at her.

She shrugged. "Two are better than one."

Conrad felt a lurch of hope inside himself. But then he told himself she didn't mean anything by her words. She was talking about a wooden garden decoration, not him.

They walked over to Conrad's car and got inside. He then backed out of his driveway and they started down the road to the freeway. The car's headlights cut a path through the black night.

"It's peaceful out here," Katrina said.

"There's not a better place to call home," Conrad said as he looked over at her. There was just enough moonlight to outline her features. Her profile reminded him of the calendar picture he'd looked at for so long. The funny thing was that, now that he'd gotten to know her, the calendar photo paled in comparison.

"You're beautiful," he said without thinking.

She looked startled.

"I mean—everything is beautiful on a night like this," Conrad said.

It was silent for a moment, and then Conrad cleared his throat. "Tracy called to say she found someone to work with Pete on your picture. Lucy Morgan, the sister to the café owner."

"Is she old enough?" Katrina asked. "Linda talks about her as if she's a child."

"She just turned twenty," Conrad said. "Maybe you can make her look older."

As he drove over the hill that led down to the freeway, the sun was starting to rise and the skyline was turning slightly pink.

"It's going to be a beautiful morning for a picture," Katrina said. "I hope Leanne gets here in time to watch us take it."

"I don't think there's any truck stops close enough for that to happen," Conrad said. "I'd guess she might get here in time for Sunday school, though. Aunt Edith said the boys are looking forward to going."

Katrina nodded. "I think Leanne would want them to go."

"But not you?" Conrad asked softly.

Katrina didn't answer and in a few minutes they were at the freeway. Conrad stepped out and went over to the sign. It was nothing more than a piece of plywood nailed to a stake made from a two-by-four. It pulled out of the ground easy enough and he put it in the trunk of his car.

He tried not to brood over Katrina's answer about Sunday school. He needed to trust God when it came to her and that was all he could do. He was well-acquainted with the wounds of the heart that she suffered. No child should ever lose a parent. It ripped something right out of them and it was hard to get it back.

He opened the door to the car and climbed back inside.

"You like being with Aunt Edith, don't you?" he asked as he turned the car around and started back to Dry Creek.

"She's wonderful," Katrina said.

"She is like a mother to everyone in Dry Creek," he said, turning the heat on in the car.

A few minutes later, he asked, "What makes you want to be a photographer?"

They spent the rest of the trip back talking about the photos she loved to take. She even pointed out a couple of shots she'd like to take.

"That sagebrush caught in those two rocks over there," Katrina said. "If a woman with red boots was sitting on top of the rock and dangling her foot down, it would be stunning."

Conrad could picture it.

"I keep lots of colors in my studio," Katrina said. "I have this filing system so I can find them."

"Like I do with my bolts," Conrad said. Maybe the two of them had more in common than he'd thought. "In my shop, I keep everything in order so I can find things easily."

They were both silent for a few minutes.

"We have a lot of good scenery around here," Conrad finally said, which was as close as he'd ever come to trying to convince a woman to stay. "The mountains and the plains—you don't get better than that for photos. Even those gullies can be striking. It all changes with the season, too, so there's lots of variety. And we've got good light all the time. It's big sky country, you know."

Katrina nodded. "The sunrise is certainly beautiful here."

Conrad decided it was time to stop telling her how wonderful Dry Creek was. He wasn't ready to suffer the disappointment when she left. And she would leave. He didn't dare hope for anything else. And he couldn't feel sorry for himself, not when he had his uncle and his friends. He had a good life. His days might not be filled with joy, but they weren't shattered with pain, either. He would have to be content with that.

Chapter Eight

The sunrise was in its full glory by the time Conrad drove them back into town. Bright pink clouds edged the eastern sky and turned the wet asphalt in front of the car a rosy color. There were no lights in any house windows yet, but a few of the dogs were starting to stir. Katrina thought she heard a rooster crowing from behind one of the houses as Conrad parked on the street by his house. She couldn't blame the rooster for greeting a morning like this with such enthusiasm.

Katrina wondered if the town had changed so much in the day she'd been here or if the change was inside her. Everything looked charming now as opposed to yesterday when she'd thought it had seemed rundown.

"I'd invite you into my house," Conrad said as he opened his car door. "But I have a construction zone going on inside." He gave her a quick grin. "I wouldn't want to scare you away. It'll look good eventually, but—"

"I don't scare easy. And I love those before and after photos. I could shoot a couple for you, if you'd like."

"That'd be great," he said as he slid out the door.

Katrina opened her door, too, and walked partially around the car to meet him.

"I need to get my camera from Leanne's car," Katrina said, knowing the gas station was just down the road from here.

He nodded. "I've got the keys with me." He reached in his pocket and pulled out Leanne's car key and another key chain that must hold his gas station keys.

He put the keys back in his pocket and put his arm around her shoulders as they started to walk.

"It's still dark enough that you might fall," was all he said by way of explanation.

Katrina wondered if he knew the fall she might take had nothing to do with her feet even though she was wearing her battered high heels. It was her heart that was already cracked and in danger of shattering completely.

"When Leanne gets here, I can at least get my tennis shoes out of the trunk of my car."

It was best that she keep herself distracted. She wished she could pretend, just for a little while, that things would work out between her and Conrad, but nothing but sadness would come from letting her imagination go in that direction. She was a realist. If God didn't save her parents, there was no guarantee He'd spare her from cancer. She couldn't ask Conrad to suffer with her. He'd been so devastated by his mother's death. How would he handle her illness?

She took a step that put a little distance between them. He had to move his arm anyway because they were at the office door of his gas station and he needed to get the key out.

"When should we be ready for the photo shoot?" she asked as they stood there.

She needed to keep moving through this day and stop thinking about what might have been or could be if nothing else happened to stop it.

"Everyone's supposed to be there just after dawn," Conrad said as he slipped the key into the lock. "I'd say another fifteen minutes. Tracy made all the arrangements and she called Pete and told him to be early."

Katrina smiled. "She probably has him running laps around that sign now just to make him suffer."

Conrad turned the key in the lock and gave the door a push. The inside of the station was dark until Conrad flipped a light switch. Then he led the way into his office.

"We should call and leave a message for the sheriff to let him know that Leanne called you," Conrad said as he walked over to his desk and opened a drawer. "I have his office number here. No need to call the phone he keeps by his bed in case of emergencies. There's nothing he can do until later this morning anyway."

Conrad pulled a small notebook out of the top drawer and flipped a couple of pages. "Here it is. Do you want to call?"

"Sure, although there's not much I can tell him except that Leanne's heading this way and is trying to stay away from Walker." Katrina dialed the number Conrad had pointed to on the page. "But I'd like him to hear it from me first."

"He'll want to call back and talk to you

anyway," Conrad said. "He knows you're staying with my aunt and uncle so he'll call before church. Either that or talk to you there. He and his wife, Barbara, usually help with one of the Sunday school classes."

Katrina left her message on the sheriff's voice mail and hung up. "Now that Leanne called, I must be in the clear as far as the law is concerned," she said.

"That's right," Conrad said as he pulled the keys for Leanne's car out of his pocket and started walking to door leading to the garage.

"You'll have to jiggle that key in the trunk," Katrina said as she followed him. "It took me five minutes to get it open yesterday. You press it hard to the left and then back right sort of easy."

"I'm a master with keys,"

Conrad opened the door leading to the garage for Katrina. "Even Houdini couldn't break in here. You have to unlock the main door with this hidden button." He pushed something on top of the doorjamb and the large door began to move. "That way no one can just break a window and come in and back out a car I'm working on. I don't keep any money here at night, but I sleep better knowing

I've protected my customers' property the best I can."

Katrina nodded as he pushed the button again and the door came back down. They walked over to the car sitting in the middle of the garage. Conrad slipped the key into the trunk slot of Leanne's car and two seconds later there was a slight pop and he pulled the trunk open and bowed. "Voila. The master at work."

"I'm impressed," Katrina said with a smile. "But the real trick is to find the right bag. I have my camera in a black bag with a reflective strip sewn on the back. It shines yellow."

"There have to be half a dozen black bags in here," he said.

Katrina smiled. "There're not all mine, but most of them are. I use one for my film. Another for my batteries and lenses. And, of course, one for my main camera. Oh, another for my backup camera. Usually I travel with a developing kit but that's still in the Lexus. I think it's that one." She pointed at a bag.

"I've got it," Conrad said as he held the right bag up.

"That's it. Thanks. I'll wait until we get to your house before I open it, though. I wouldn't want to lose anything in here and have to come back for it later."

They went back through the office and out that door again. Conrad turned the lock and put the station key, along with Leanne's key, back in his pocket.

"I should make some coffee when we're at my place," he said as they walked down the street. "That might keep Pete happier."

"Unless I'm a poor judge of the way things are, Tracy will have made some for him," Katrina said.

Conrad had given her his arm automatically when they started their walk down here and she'd accepted it without comment. Sometimes people just did things for those they cared about without even seeming to be aware of it. Like Tracy making coffee for Pete. Not that, Katrina reminded herself, she and Conrad were—well, they weren't like Tracy and Pete.

Katrina noticed there was a nice, golden cast to the morning. "It's going to be a good day for pictures."

She needed to keep herself focused. Until she knew just how sick she was, she needed to keep lots of space between her and Conrad. Together, they stepped up on his porch.

* * *

Conrad self-consciously wiped his feet on the burlap sack he kept by the front door of his house. He always made sure his shoes weren't muddy when he went inside even though it might seem unnecessary to most people. "The floors are still plywood. I ripped them up because I had to rebuild some of the supports."

Ever since he bought this old house, Conrad had treated it with respect. He didn't want to wait until he had the expensive flooring to live the way he planned to in this place. When he first saw the rundown house, he knew it had once been a happy home and could be again, someday. He liked knowing he was making that kind of difference.

Katrina wiped the soles of her high heels as he opened the door.

Conrad almost breathed a sigh of relief. Not everyone saw the house the way he did. The sunlight was being kind to him. The living room had large paned windows on three sides. The sills on the old windows had partially rotted from moisture over the years and he'd considered replacing them with the modern single pane ones with the hard plastic casings, but then he'd found a restoration catalogue and ordered rebuilt windows. It gave the room the look of an English cottage, especially with the fireplace he had partially finished along the long left-hand side of the room. He'd found country rocks to use in the fireplace and a solid length of oak to use as a mantel.

"I'm going to put an oak wood floor in here," he said. "And then have area rugs. I've painted everything white for now, but I might add some color when I finish up everything."

"It's the most peaceful room I've ever seen," Katrina said.

Conrad smiled. She sounded sincere.

"I'm going to plant more trees outside, too."

They walked a little farther. "I wanted slate floor in the kitchen, but I need to get the plumbing finished first. It's an old house and it wasn't set up for a dishwasher and an icemaker on the refrigerator."

"You've already got the stove, though," Katrina noted as she walked over to the double-oven appliance. "You even have a grill in it. I've seen these in the gourmet food magazines."

"I don't cook much," Conrad said. "But I'm hoping this might inspire me to learn."

Katrina took a few steps farther and stopped. Conrad was following right behind her. He liked letting her discover his house at her own pace.

"This has got to be the family room," she said. "All of those built-in shelves along one wall. You could put overstuffed chairs in front of the shelves, which would, of course, have family photos and books lined up on them. There's so much light coming in it's a great place to read."

He nodded. "I thought I might add a drafting table, too. For when I want to—" He stopped. Linda would not approve, but he continued. "For when I want to draw the inside of engines. All kinds of engines. I like to do that sometimes."

Conrad held his breath, but Katrina didn't look dismayed or anything. The café owner must be wrong about women thinking that sounded boring.

"You'll want to get a chair that's the right height to go with the table," was all she said. "I imagine you could spend hours working there."

Conrad felt the breath ease out of him.

"I turned two of the bedrooms into a large one," he said as they walked farther into the house. "I haven't done much in the room yet, but I plan to have a sleeping area and then a sitting area in the alcove so people can talk together in the evenings if they want."

Katrina looked around the room and then nodded her approval. "If you put hardwood floors in here it would be big enough for dancing. Even when you've got the furniture in place."

Conrad hadn't blushed since he was eleven years old, but he felt the heat sweep up his face. The image of Katrina in her nightgown swirling around the room with him was more than he could calmly take.

He managed to clear his throat and said, "I am planning on wood floors."

"Good," was all she said to that.

He wondered if he imagined the satisfaction in her voice, but he didn't have the nerve to ask her about it. What could he say anyway? If she wasn't willing to date him, it stood to reason she was miles away from agreeing to anything more.

After they left the bedroom, Katrina got her camera out of the bag and set to taking photos of his house. The living room, the kitchen, the bedroom—she shot them all from slightly different angles.

Fortunately, she didn't require much in the way of conversation from him.

When Katrina finished with her pictures, she put her camera back in the bag and he picked it up to carry for her just like his whole world wasn't changing as they spent more time together.

He was beginning to believe God could be moving in his life. Maybe Katrina would come to church with him this morning. Maybe she would realize God loved her. Maybe the two of them could get to know each other better and eventually, well, go dancing in his bedroom as man and wife.

Conrad stopped himself. The very thought of getting married made him feel as if he was standing on the edge of a cliff. He wasn't sure he had what it took to love someone until death did them part. And it wasn't just death. So many things could happen. He'd never realized the courage of ordinary men like his uncle.

Katrina carried the inside of Conrad's house in her mind as they left. She planned to make double copies of those photographs so she'd have something to remember. She'd even managed to get Conrad in a couple of the shots. He hadn't realized she was taking his picture along with the rooms of his house. She planned to hold on to these photos and bring them out whenever she started to miss him.

She promised herself she wouldn't cry, but she would remember him all the same. It would be best for him if she stayed away until she knew whether her cancer was gone. But she would miss him all the same.

The light had turned a little whiter as they walked down the street. The golden glow had lessened some, but the overall quality of the light was better. The dampness was beginning to dry off of the asphalt and Katrina could walk better in her heels. She was relieved because she didn't want to run around town barefoot.

As they neared the bent stop sign, a couple of old pickups pulled onto the gravel road that crossed the asphalt. High weeds lined the sides of both roads.

A young blonde woman stepped out of one of the vehicles and Katrina wished she had an electric fan. The woman must be

Lucy and she had long blond hair that shone in the sunlight. If they could make it look as if the wind was blowing, Lucy and her hair would make as striking a photo as any of the women Katrina had used from the modeling agency in Los Angeles.

Just then the doors to the other pickup opened and Tracy and Pete got out their respective doors.

"Oh, no," Katrina said. She couldn't hear what the two were saying, but they were clearly arguing.

"We better get over there," Conrad said as he picked up their pace.

They were a few yards away when they first heard the words being shouted.

"It was not an insult," Pete yelled. He was as indignant as a barnyard rooster. "It was a kiss!"

With that declaration, everyone was stunned into silence. Katrina looked over at Conrad, but he looked as confused as she felt.

"I gave you a thermos of coffee," Tracy finally said, her voice strained. She looked at Pete and then turned to Katrina to explain. "It was just a simple gesture of goodwill because he was taking *your* picture. He didn't need to kiss me."

"I see," Katrina said although in truth she didn't really understand anything except that it was apparently all her fault. Then she noticed that Tracy looked as if she might cry at any minute. "We may as well get started."

Katrina hoped to get everyone so busy that no one would notice the tears forming in the other woman's eyes.

"Ah, I'm sorry," Pete said and he looked down at his boots. "I shouldn't have bitten your head off just because you gave my face a little slap. I've had worse." He paused a second and then added, "Although not because I've kissed anyone. Usually, I've been slapped for not kissing them."

"I find that hard to believe," Tracy snapped. Her lips pinched together, but at least she had control of her tears.

"I'm sure you do, ma'am," the ranch hand said and, with that, he reached back into the pickup and pulled out his Stetson.

"I'm ready when you are," Pete said as he pushed the Stetson down on his head.

Katrina nodded and started to think of where everyone should stand. She liked nothing better than staging a photograph. She could imagine what it would be like with the light hitting it this way and that way. She'd ask for a full smile from one model and a half smile from another. She'd move an arm or a foot. Sometimes she'd shift a prop. Although with the stop sign, she'd have to move the models around it instead of moving the sign.

"Just so everyone knows," she said. "This is not a digital camera. So you won't be able to see your pictures right away. I'll have to develop them."

Once she started taking pictures, she wasn't distracted by the people watching her. Not even Pete and Tracy, who were standing so far apart they were clearly trying to show they were not together, could break her concentration, although they kept glaring at each other, which pretty much said they had to be together. And then there was Conrad, who she didn't have time to think about—not now, anyway. Maybe when she'd finished the photos she'd have time to sort him out in her mind.

Chapter Nine

Katrina took the last photo. She had ones of Lucy smiling up at Pete and of him looking down at her with a smoldering look in his eyes that seemed a little maniacal to Katrina. Of course, that might only be because Lucy couldn't seem to look at Pete without being afraid. The whole setup came out more like Little Red Riding Hood and the Big Bad Wolf, rather than two people in love.

"I don't think any of these pictures will work," Katrina whispered to Conrad who was standing beside her. "It's the—"

"The look in their eyes," Conrad finished for her.

She nodded and continued in a whisper. "Maybe we should have Pete put his hat back on. Then we won't see his eyes."

"But we'd still see Lucy's. You'd think you were asking her to look at a grizzly bear instead of some harmless ranch hand."

Katrina lifted her eyebrow. "He didn't sound harmless when he was yelling."

"Maybe Tracy can show her how it's done," Conrad said.

"No, I—" Katrina started to say, but Conrad was already walking over to the woman. Well, it couldn't be any worse than it was now, she finally decided.

"Just relax your shoulders," Katrina said as Tracy walked over hesitantly. "Imagine you're on some beach in Fiji with the breeze blowing in your hair and the flowers swaying and—"

Pete snorted. "Her and her big city places. Nothing around here is ever good enough for her. She has to go running off to the bright lights."

"I came back, didn't I?" Tracy had bright red spots on her cheeks. "And what do you care about where I've been?"

Now, Katrina had to figure out how to calm Tracy down.

"Coming home is good," Katrina said with a smile for the other woman.

"Oh, she did that, all right," Pete muttered under his breath.

"Look—" Katrina spun around to face the ranch hand and she saw that his face was pale. "Are you okay?"

"Of course, I'm okay," he snapped back.

Katrina looked at him in dismay. "Maybe it's too much to ask. We're just trying to show Lucy how two mature adults can look at each other with admiration and affection when they need to—" Katrina stopped.

Pete's color had come back and so had his attitude.

Just then Conrad stepped up and put his hand on Pete's shoulder. "If you need to think of something, remember that knocking sound in your pickup. Pretend you're looking at the mechanic who's going to fix it for free if you pull this picture off looking like a reasonable human being."

Pete looked at Conrad for a long minute and then nodded.

"I am reasonable," he said calmly as he walked back to the sign and gestured for Tracy to follow him. "Come on, let's get this over with."

Katrina figured that probably wasn't the best way to stage a romantic picture, but if it worked for the two of them, she'd be there to shoot it.

She had her eye to the camera when she noticed that things were going terribly wrong. The look of wretched hopelessness on Pete's and Tracy's faces stunned Katrina.

She took the shot before she thought too much about what all that meant. She could never use that picture, of course. The emotions it showed were too raw. The two of them had heart, but it wasn't the calm, pretty kind of heart she figured the calendar people would want.

"Well," Katrina said as she stepped away. She tried to keep her voice even so she wouldn't give anything away. The two might not realize what their faces showed. "That one we won't use, but maybe Lucy—could you stand where Tracy is? Maybe we can get another one at that angle."

"Can I have one of me and Ben, too?" Lucy asked shyly. "When we're finished with the real pictures, I mean."

Katrina nodded. "Sure. I'll shoot a couple of them for you."

She looked over at the young man who had been patient while his girlfriend gazed into Pete's face. He didn't look at all jealous. Of course, Katrina couldn't fault him for that. Lucy certainly hadn't managed to look smitten with the ranch hand. Both Lucy and her boyfriend looked so unbearably young, though, as if life hadn't touched them yet with any of the other problems that tormented people like Tracy and Pete.

Katrina looked back at the couple in their forties. She wondered what was keeping them apart. Or if they even knew they were in love.

Conrad hung back so he could help Katrina finish what she needed to do with her photo shoot. He'd been impressed by how good she was at setting up her pictures. Even he could tell that she tried some innovative angles. And the way she used that rusted old signpost to balance everything in her pictures was amazing.

She was also very kind to Lucy and Pete, promising them payment for their photos if she was able to sell them for the calendar. The ranch hand snorted when she said the calendar was Romance Across America, but Conrad noticed he didn't say no when Katrina offered to pay him if the picture was used.

"Maybe I'll hire you to shoot some pictures of my gas station," Conrad said as Katrina zipped up the bag with her camera inside. "I could use them when I want to run an ad in the newspaper."

"Sure." She smiled. "I can focus on your clean windows. I'm sure your customers appreciate knowing you take such care of your building and their cars."

"I could come up with a new slogan," he said as he reached out to lift her bag. It wasn't heavy, but he could carry it on his shoulder easier than she could on hers, if for no other reason than that he was wearing boots and she was wearing those black high heels that didn't provide an ounce of support.

He offered his arm and Katrina took it without even breaking her stride, which made him feel good.

"The only photo I took that shows any kind of love is that one of Tracy and Pete," Katrina said as they walked back toward his gas station. "And I didn't do anything to make it happen."

"You shot the picture," he protested as they stepped up on the asphalt road. The ground was firmer than it had been yesterday. Maybe it was finally drying out.

"No, I mean—I like to set the picture up. The angle that the woman is leaning in, the distance everything is from the camera lens. But the anguish on their faces. I'm just not comfortable with such strong emotions being out there for everyone to see."

"I respect you for leaving them their privacy," Conrad protested. "That's not wrong, it's—"

"I'm not saying I regret that," Katrina said. She kept her eyes on the ground and Conrad didn't think it was because she was worried about falling. "I'm saying I wonder if it's going to stop me from being a good photographer."

Conrad stopped. They were across from where the church stood. Lights were on in the building, but Sunday school wouldn't start for another hour.

Katrina looked up at him when he stopped. "My sister used to say I needed to express my feelings. I try, but it's like something blocks them. I wonder if that affects my photos. Maybe that's why the calendar people didn't buy any of the pictures I sent. Maybe that's why my pictures didn't have heart."

"You're a great photographer," he said as he looked her square in the eyes. "I'm sure the calendar people probably do want pictures with lots of emotions, but those feelings don't all need to be painful ones. There are good emotions, too. Like joy. Contentment. Excitement."

"I guess," Katrina said without much conviction.

Conrad took in a breath. "I'm not always comfortable with strong emotions, either. I think I may have burned out when my mom died. For years, I didn't even like Christmas. Or birthday parties. Or anything. I just wanted peace. Every time the other kids were happy, I was worried something awful was going to happen."

Since yesterday morning, Conrad had told Katrina more about himself than he'd ever told anyone. Not that people hadn't guessed how difficult things had been when he was a child. But he hadn't said anything. He knew the risk he was taking. Katrina might leave when her sister got here. All of the secrets he told her would make him miss her more if she left.

They walked in silence for the last few minutes until they reached his uncle's house. Conrad wiped his feet on the outside welcome mat and then opened the door. The faint smell of gingerbread still filled the house.

"I could fix us some coffee," he offered as he stepped into the entryway. "We've already had quite the morning and you haven't even told me everything your sister said yet."

Katrina followed him inside the house. "She didn't really say much. It was the tone of her voice that worried me more than anything."

Conrad sat the camera bag down on a table beside the door. Daylight was just beginning to seep into the room, but it was still dark. He walked over and turned on a floor lamp that stood by the sofa. Suddenly, he could see everything.

"Oh, I should—" He grabbed the gray wool blanket he'd used for his bed last night and started to fold it.

"Here. Let me help," Katrina said as she took one end of the blanket. Together they shook it out and started to match up the correct corners.

"Thanks," Conrad said. "Aunt Edith likes a tidy house."

They folded the blanket in silence.

"I wonder what went wrong with my sister and her husband," Katrina finally said. "I know they loved each other when they got married. I heard it in Leanne's voice when she told me about Walker back then. I was half jealous that she had someone she felt that way about. And it seemed like he felt the same way."

Conrad took the folded blanket and set it on the back of the sofa. Then he sat down and gestured for Katrina to sit as well.

"How does she feel now?" Conrad asked.

"She's scared of him. And surprised, I think. She told me she'd been the one to buy the car. She'd worked in some grocery store for a few weeks and used that money to buy it."

"I suppose things change. Maybe he's worried he was losing her."

Katrina shook her head. "He's the one having an affair—at least I think he's having one. He stays out all night sometimes and doesn't tell Leanne where he's been."

"Did you tell the sheriff about that? I wonder if the other woman was the one who trashed the house then."

"I'll mention it to him. It might even

explain the remark about Leanne needing to leave or she'd be hurt."

Just then they both heard tiny footsteps upstairs.

"Someone's up," Conrad said as the boys started down the stairs.

They were sleepy and Katrina opened her arms to them. They both came to sit by her. Katrina patted each boy on the head. Then she said, "I talked to your mom and she wanted me to give you her love. And a kiss."

With that, Katrina kissed both boys on the cheek.

They were still so sleepy, they just yawned. Which made her want to hug them again. They hadn't even considered that their mother might be in danger.

That's the way it should be, though, she told herself.

The next person down the stairs was Charley. He was pulling up his suspenders. Katrina knew he didn't see her and Conrad until he reached the bottom of the stairs, because he stopped when he did notice them and a big grin spread over his face.

"Good to see you both up," he said. "I'll just take the boys into the kitchen so the two of you can talk."

Katrina laughed. "We've already solved the problems of the world."

"And we have good news," Conrad added. "Leanne called. She's supposed to be on her way here."

"Well, this calls for a celebration," the older man said. "And I happen to know Edith is on her way down to fix us all waffles. Maybe she'll give us some of her chokecherry syrup. She hoards that for special occasions."

When Edith came down the stairs, tying her apron over her Sunday dress, Katrina stood up.

"Is there anything I can do to help with breakfast?" she asked.

Edith answered as she walked through the living room. "Come with me. You can get the jar of syrup off the shelf in the pantry. That's always too high for me and my daughter, Doris, fusses if I use a stepladder."

Katrina nodded.

Fifteen minutes later, they were all sitting down to bacon and waffles with Edith's chokecherry syrup. Katrina had never tasted anything so heavenly.

After several waffles each, Charley put his fork down and smiled at his wife. "Is it any wonder I'm in love?"

"Oh, you—" Edith protested. "You ate my cooking for years before you married me and you could have eaten it for the rest of your life without saying a word to me about being married. You proposed to me for love and nothing else."

"I sure did," Charley teased her. "I'd have married you if all you could make was burnt toast."

"Well, fortunately, we're not reduced to that," the older woman said as she finished her waffle.

Katrina felt lonely. Suddenly, she didn't want to put her life on hold while some disease decided whether she would live or not.

She put her fork down. "There's something I need to tell everyone."

They all set their forks down, too, and looked at her. She saw the happy flush on Edith's face and the quiet affection in Charley's eyes. There was something unreadable in Conrad's eyes that made her nervous. Her two nephews looked mildly curious.

Katrina wanted to share her burden. But the words wouldn't come out of her mouth. It suddenly occurred to her that, if she finally said the words, a whole rush of emotion would come out of her with them. Sadness. Anger. Resentment. Both for the cancer and for all the hurts in her childhood.

That wouldn't make for a happy breakfast.

"I wanted to thank everyone for worrying about my sister," she finally mumbled. She couldn't tell them about the cancer. Not yet.

"We're pleased she's okay," Charley said.

Edith and Conrad nodded.

"We want you to tell her she's welcome to stay with us, too," Edith added. "Until she feels ready to go home."

"Thank you," Katrina said.

"Well, we better get moving if we want to be on time for Sunday school," Edith said as she pushed back her chair and looked at the boys. "It should be a beautiful day."

Katrina opened her mouth and closed it again. Maybe when her sister was here, she could tell everyone about her health. There was no reason to have to repeat herself anyway. In the meantime, she had to figure out how to cope with church.

Her old vow that she'd never set foot in a church was complicated for her now. Her nephews would be inside the church; they certainly had nothing against God. Suddenly, she wondered if it was wise to keep her vow. In all the years she'd avoided churches, God hadn't seemed to suffer. Instead it was her who felt left out, not Him.

"Oh, you'll need money for the collection plate," she suddenly remembered and looked at her nephews. She used to love giving her dimes as the plate was passed around. "I'll get some for you."

Katrina stood up and walked over to the table where she'd put her purse. She opened up her wallet and brought out two dollar bills. She walked back and gave one each to her nephews.

"Usually, the kids only give quarters in Sunday school," Edith said.

"That's okay," Katrina said. She wanted her nephews to feel as if they belonged.

Katrina glanced over at Conrad and saw he was looking at her with approval. She didn't want him to misinterpret her actions, though. "It's just a few dollars. They probably use it to buy materials anyway."

"The Sunday school offering is going to Africa this month," Edith said proudly and then she realized. "Oh, dear. I'm sorry." She looked at Katrina. "I didn't think—"

"That's all right," Katrina said, even though it wasn't.

"Maybe the boys should save their dollars for next month. It's camp then," Edith said in a rush. "In the foothills of the Tetons. It's a lovely place for children."

"The money can go to Africa," Katrina assured her. "The boys didn't even know my parents."

Which, she realized, was an added bitterness. Her parents would have loved to know their grandchildren. But no sooner had that thought hit her than she realized that her parents would not only have wanted them to go to Sunday school, but they would have wanted the boys to give all they could to African missions as well.

Chapter Ten

Katrina was embarrassed. She might as well be sitting beside the fold-out table on the church porch with a scarlet H branded on her forehead for 'heathen.' The fact that she was wearing the only pair of shoes she had with her, these muddy high heels, didn't make it any easier. All of the other women were wearing boots or tennis shoes. She even saw some old-fashioned galoshes.

"Everybody's asking why we're sitting out here instead of inside," Katrina whispered to Conrad as they sat beside a fold-out table on the church porch.

"It's a great gimmick, isn't it?" Conrad said cheerfully. "Aunt Edith is going to be pleased. Everyone is stopping by to sign up for their directory photos."

"They're not stopping by. We're blocking the door and you won't let them through until they pick a time to have their picture taken."

Conrad grinned. "Works like a charm."

"And," she continued indignantly, "one woman whispered in my ear that I should leave my shoes at the altar. What does she think I'm going to walk in?"

"I could always carry you where you need to go."

"Oh, that would work," Katrina muttered. "Then she'd tell me to leave you on the altar."

She finally heard what she said and the realization sucked the air out of her. She wondered if people still did that? Take the thing they wanted the most in the world and set it before God? Well, she sure wasn't going to wait around to find out. She had agreed to help with the appointments for the church directory because she'd already said she would help. But that was a business decision. It had nothing to do with altars and giving everything up. Besides, most altars were not real anymore; it was just a place up front where people stood to pray.

With another stab of memory, she recalled when her parents had gone up to the altar before they went on their missionary trip. They'd said they'd give everything to God, holding nothing back. They'd had tears of happiness on their faces. She'd been happy, too, that night. It had all seemed like a great adventure.

"Could we have our pictures taken with Clarence?" an older woman asked. She and an older man had just arrived at the table and were out of breath from climbing the steps. She had a little black hat on her head with a puff of netting that hung over her lined face. "He's not a member of the church, of course, but he's a member of our family and—"

"I don't—" Conrad started.

"Most churches include children," Katrina protested. They looked like such a sweet couple. A woman who still wore hats had to have class. "Is he your grandson?"

"He's a snake," Conrad said. "Garden variety."

"Oh."

"We keep him around to remind us of the Great Temptation," the older man said. He'd had a bit of a struggle to stop wheezing, but he was back to normal. He didn't wear a hat, but his shoes had been recently polished.

"Clarence is quite well behaved," the

woman assured them. "He'd be no problem in a picture."

Katrina looked at Conrad, but he deferred to her.

"I'm sorry, but I think we need to limit the photos to humans," Katrina said with her best smile. "I know you're very fond of Clarence and I'm sure he—ah—has a certain amount of affection for you, too, but—"

"He'll be very disappointed," the woman said as she looked at the schedule Conrad had lifted up to her. "We'll take Tuesday at ten in the morning. He's sleeping then so he won't miss us as much."

Conrad nodded. "Come here to the church," he said, writing their names on his schedule.

"On the steps," Katrina said. "We'll take the pictures on the steps."

"The light is better outside," Conrad added when they looked puzzled.

"And wear color." Katrina smiled as the couple opened the door to go inside the church.

"I can tell you already, we're going to have too many white shirts," Katrina said as they waited for someone else to walk by and sign up. "All of the men here are wearing white shirts. Or plaid flannel ones in navy or forest green. I hope that doesn't mean that's all they have in their closets."

Conrad nodded. "It probably is. Everyone has both, but the guys wearing flannel now are the ones who think winter is going to hang around for a while. The white cotton guys believe spring has to be here somewhere so they're dressing for it whether they freeze doing it or not. It's a sign of hope."

Conrad looked down at his own white shirt and patted his sleeves. "Some guys buy the snapped kind, but I go with the old-fashioned buttons."

"The weather doesn't go by a shirt," Katrina said as she shook her head. "Besides, the best color for photographs is usually blue."

Another couple was walking up the steps so they both focused their attention on them.

"Photos for the church directory," Conrad said as he lifted up the scheduling sheet. "What time works for you?"

Conrad signed them up and let them go on their way.

She and Conrad had spent twenty minutes here on the porch so far and, according to him, church was going to start in ten minutes.

"I can sit out here and get the latecomers," she whispered to him. "You go in and enjoy the service."

"No, I've got it figured out. Besides, we want everyone in that directory," he said.

Just then a bell rang. It was the kind of sound a librarian's bell would make.

"Sunday school is over," Conrad announced. "I could go get you a cup of coffee if you'd like. They probably have those little doughnuts, too."

"I don't need a doughnut, but I wouldn't mind some coffee."

Conrad nodded and stood up from his folding chair. "Just have people fill in the time slot they want. I'll be back so quick you won't know I was gone."

Of course, Katrina told herself five minutes later, that wasn't true at all. She was flooded with questions and she didn't know half of the answers. She knew Conrad was gone all right.

"I'm pretty sure the restrooms are inside the building somewhere." Katrina figured she'd start with the easiest questions first. "About the toupee—I would say that if you normally wear it, then use it in the picture. If you don't, then don't. The rest of the questions will have to wait for Conrad to get back."

Katrina told herself the seven old men who'd gathered around her table would have to be content with those answers to their questions.

"What I want to know," a wrinkled old man with a baseball cap on his head and tennis shoes on his feet said, "is whether or not you're Conrad's wife. The one we've been praying for."

"Conrad isn't married," she said gently. She wondered if the old man was generally confused.

"Well, of course not yet—" the man said before he was interrupted.

"Don't mind Harry," one of the old men apologized.

"He's—" Yet another one of them searched for words. "He talks too much."

It wasn't until they were all gone that Katrina realized none of them had signed up to get their picture taken for the church directory. Well, Conrad would have to chase them down. Maybe his uncle could help.

A piano was playing some of the old

hymns Katrina remembered before Conrad opened the door. He held out a cup of coffee to her. "People inside had questions about their pictures."

Katrina took the cup. "I meant it when I said I'd sit here if you want to go. I know you won't want to miss the sermon."

Conrad grinned. "I have a plan."

With that he opened the door slightly. "We'll be able to hear just fine out here."

The people inside the church were standing to sing "Amazing Grace."

Conrad stood, so she did as well. She had to admit it was strange to be going to church without being in the actual room with everyone else. It was sort of freeing in a way. She could be a spectator instead of a participant.

For such a small group of people, they managed to sing together pretty well. Conrad had a nice deep voice, too, and he sang with feeling.

Going to church this way wasn't going to be too bad, she decided.

Fifteen minutes later she was sitting in her folding chair and sobbing. She had just bullied Conrad into going back inside to get her more coffee so she could cry without him seeing her. He would take the tears all the wrong way and she didn't want him to be disappointed. She wasn't weeping about God; her tears were coming because she had so much wrong with her life and He wasn't any comfort to her at all.

If she was going to design a perfect God, He certainly wasn't it. He didn't seem to understand that He owed her. He had taken her parents; He should have some special something for her. And yet here she sat, wondering if she'd be forced to go back to a job she hated or if she was going to die from cancer or if she'd see her sister happy again.

The door that Conrad had opened slightly before now swung wider.

Katrina put her head down. Her hair was long enough to hide her face. She just needed to get her breathing under control. She put her one elbow on the foldout table and, with the other arm, pushed the scheduling sheets to the corner so she didn't smear any names.

Conrad set down a cup of coffee in front of her. A second later he set down a box of tissues with tiny yellow flowers. She recognized the box.

"What? Do you carry them around with

you?" she asked incredulously, her voice still thick with the tears.

Conrad shook his head. "I buy them wholesale and give a few boxes to the church. I thought you might want some. I need to order soon again anyway."

"My life's a mess," she said as she reached for one. "I need more than a tissue."

He nodded. "You need God. But I figure you're realizing that in your own way."

She didn't say anything for a minute. Then it just came out. "I could be dying, you know."

"What?" The smile froze on Conrad's face and it was still there even though his eyes were shocked. "You don't mean—"

She nodded her head. "I might die."

"But—" he protested.

"I figured you should know," she said and then she took another tissue. "I'll know for sure in four months, two weeks and four days. That's my next appointment with the oncologist."

"Cancer?" he asked, his voice strained.

She nodded and dabbed at her eyes. "That's why I can't seem to stop crying. I don't know what's going to happen. I had surgery, but the doctor won't give me an all-clear yet."

"I just can't believe it," he finally said.

"Welcome to the club," she said and with that she stood up and began to walk down the steps. She had to go slowly because her tears kept making her vision blurry and she didn't want to stumble in her heels.

"I'm going to go sit in Leanne's car," she said loud enough for him to hear if he wanted. She didn't turn around, though.

It wasn't until she was almost to the gas station that she remembered everything there was locked up tight so she couldn't get inside to sit in the car. Oh, well, she thought as she took the final steps and sat down on the concrete slab by the gas pumps. At least that overhang gave her a covering in case the clouds in the sky turned to rain. The way she felt now, she didn't care if she got soaked. She was miserable anyway.

Conrad watched his future walk away from him and he didn't know what to do to get it back. If Katrina had given him some ordinary reasons why she didn't think they could be together, he could have reasoned with her point by point.

But what could he say to cancer?

He had known when he saw Katrina tear up a few minutes ago, after the pastor made those remarks about hope, that she was close to forging a truce with God. It might take her some time to admit that He loved her, but she knew. In her heart, she knew.

Conrad had been happy because she would be happier someday.

But this—he couldn't keep falling in love with her if she was going to die. He wouldn't put himself through what his father had endured. He needed to pull his heart back from the brink.

He had watched Katrina as she walked down the street to the gas station. He should have given her the key to her sister's car. It was right here in his pocket.

When he saw her reach his gas station and sit down on the concrete, leaning against one of his pumps, he felt his misery deepen. This must have been why she said she couldn't date him. Why hadn't he left well enough alone?

It was that prayer request of his uncle's that had started it all. It had made Conrad long for things he shouldn't.

The congregation was standing to sing the last hymn of the day and Conrad stood with them. It was habit. He didn't join in the singing; he didn't even hear the words.

Katrina counted two cracks in the concrete slab that fronted Conrad's gas station. The slab was fairly new so she guessed the icy weather had caused them. She had her leather jacket pulled tight to her shoulders, but she wasn't cold. She was afraid. She was like that concrete. The words of the sermon had started a crack in her and she didn't know how to stop it. She'd known she should avoid thinking about God. The tears had slowed to a drip, but she still felt the emotions rushing out of some deep place inside her. She'd been able to contain them until now. Maybe this was why she didn't like those strong feelings in her photos. She couldn't control them in her life, not if she let them free.

She wrapped her arms around her knees and buried her head in the circle her arms created. She stayed that way for a long time. Then she heard the soft shuffle of footsteps coming toward her. She didn't want anyone to see the tear streaks on her face so she didn't raise her head. Whoever it was would go away, she figured.

Then she felt a hand caress her head. She could see enough through the tangle of her elbows and knees to see a pair of white orthopedic shoes.

"Edith," Katrina said. Her throat was raw and she needed a tissue. "I can't talk."

"I'll just sit with you then," Edith said, her voice warm with love.

Katrina didn't say anything for a bit and then she realized Edith couldn't sit here. It was enough to make her look up.

"But this is concrete," she protested. "You could break something trying to—" She saw her friend begin her descent anyway.

"Oh, here." Katrina put her arms up to help the older woman finish coming down.

Edith had a thick coat on and it must have had a big pocket because she pulled a handful of tissues out of it. "Conrad sent these over. I didn't have room for the box."

Katrina reached over and took the tissues. "I don't usually cry like this, it's just—"

"I know," Edith said. "Conrad told me."

Katrina shook her head. "I'm kind of used to waiting to hear about the cancer. It was the sermon today that got to me. I never should have gotten that close to a church. At least, not when it was being used."

Edith smiled. "God is Someone to be reckoned with all right."

"He should mind His own business," Katrina snapped as she dabbed away at her cheeks. Then she looked over at her friend. She couldn't believe the older woman had sat down with her; no one had cared enough to do that in a long time. "I've been thinking that it's not God I'm mad at so much. It's me. It's always been me."

"You?" Edith asked.

Katrina nodded. "I was excited for my parents to go on their mission trip. They seemed so happy and everyone in the church made such a fuss over them. I felt special just being their daughter. But then I thought I was old enough, I should have known something horrible could happen. I used to think if I had been upset, if I had begged them not to go, they wouldn't have gone. My sister was too young. She wouldn't have known anything about the bad things that could happen. But for a long time, I thought I should have known for all of us. I felt it was my fault Leanne had to grow up without our parents. No wonder we don't get along. It's always been there between us. I tried to take their place at first, but I couldn't."

"Oh, child," Edith murmured. "It wasn't your fault. None of us know the future."

"It still feels that way," Katrina said. "I could have changed everything. If only I'd asked them not to go."

"Hush now," Edith said and put her arms around Katrina.

Gradually, she rested against the older woman's shoulder. They sat that way for several minutes. Light rain was starting to fall and the sky had grown dark. A light wind was blowing through, too.

"Do you mind if I pray for you about this?" Edith asked finally. "I'll understand if you don't want me to, but God can—"

"I know," Katrina said as she sat up straighter. "And, no, I don't mind. I think it's time I made my peace with Him anyway."

"He does love you," Edith agreed softly. "You're His precious child. He wept when you wept."

For the first time in many years, Katrina could hear those words and not feel the protest growing inside her.

"Maybe He does love me." She accepted the words for the gift they were.

As the two women sat there, with their heads bowed and their hands clasped together, Katrina knew peace. Just telling someone was healing. She had come home. What had been lost to her was restored. Maybe now she'd be able to join a church family again. She'd sorely missed having one. She'd even give up her vow of not going inside a church.

And then she remembered.

"I'm sorry if Conrad was upset," Katrina said stiffly. She hadn't expected him to stand with her. Not really. Not when she might be sick.

"Give him some time," Edith said softly. "He just can't—"

"I know," Katrina said as she got her legs untangled and stood up. She held out a hand to help Edith up. "And it's all right."

The words sounded hollow to her ears; she didn't have the nerve to look at Edith's expression to see if the older woman believed her. She hadn't really expected to find a man who loved her here. Maybe it was enough that God cared. Maybe, after she talked to the doctor in a few months, she could come back. Maybe Conrad would come to care for her then if she'd had a good report from the doctor.

Chapter Eleven

Conrad sat at the card table in the middle of his dining room with a spoon in one hand and a can of pork and beans in the other. One of the windows was open and sawdust was blowing around. Not that he cared enough to get up and shut the window. The beans were tasteless anyway.

Conrad had left church before people had started coming out. He'd written a note telling his aunt about Katrina and saying he was sorry that he wouldn't be able to join them for Sunday dinner today. He'd collared one of the Bowman kids who was skipping out on the final hymn and asked him to give the note to Aunt Edith. Then Conrad had come back to his construction zone of a house.

He looked around. Usually, he got a great deal of satisfaction at seeing how he was remodeling this old house. He'd moved walls to make it all feel spacious; he'd opened up the windows to make it brighter. The materials he was using were all natural and he believed it would be a place of beauty and harmony someday.

He had hoped to live a long, sweet life in this house with his wife.

Now he didn't care.

He thought he heard someone walking on the plywood in the living room. He must have left his door open. That wasn't like him. The footsteps sounded like someone in boots so he wasn't surprised to see his uncle step into the room.

"Heard you passed up Edith's Sunday dinner," Uncle Charley said as he held out a plate with a napkin draped over it. "I brought you some of the fried chicken and mashes potatoes anyway. Some carrots, too. However, Edith said if you wanted a piece of the blueberry pie you would have to come over to the house and get it."

"I'll be passing on the pie then," Conrad said as he reached out and took the plate. He set it down on the table. "But thanks for this."

There was silence for a minute or two while Conrad studied his boots and his uncle took a good look at him.

Finally, Uncle Charley grunted. "You didn't even take the napkin off that dinner. Fried chicken is your favorite."

Conrad nodded.

"Listen, I know you were surprised to hear that Katrina might be sick, but—"

"I can't spend any more time around her," Conrad interrupted.

"But I thought she was the one for you. I thought you were starting to like her."

"I was." Conrad stood up in his chair and looked his uncle square in his eyes. "That's why I need to stop seeing her. What if she dies?"

"Ah," the older man said as he stepped close and put his hand on Conrad's shoulders. "I know it's hard, son. But a man can't love any woman without risking that he'll lose her. If you give your heart, it can be broken. In more ways than just someone dying. That's just the way it is in this life."

Conrad shook his head. "I'm going to ask Tracy out."

"But you don't love her."

Conrad nodded. "That's why I'm asking her out. She's safe."

He stopped looking at his uncle. He didn't like to see the distress on the man's face. He knew his uncle meant well, but there was nothing he could say to change Conrad's mind.

"Looks like it's going to rain some," Uncle Charley finally said as he started to walk back to the door. "See that you keep the windows closed here. You don't want any of your new wood to get warped."

Conrad nodded. "Thanks for the chicken."

"I'll see if Edith will relent and let me bring a piece of pie over later," the older man said as he left the room.

Conrad was relieved to be alone again. He stood up and went over to the windows. He'd close them up and then go change into his work clothes. He never worked on Sunday, but he hoped God wouldn't mind if he replaced that muffler this afternoon. Katrina's sister should be coming soon. He knew Katrina couldn't leave yet because of the church directory photos scheduled for tomorrow. But he wanted the car to be ready to go as soon as the sisters were.

He would be fine, he told himself. He might feel bad now, but his feelings couldn't have grown that deep. Not in a couple of days. In a few months, he'd be back to normal. Everything would be okay. His calendar woman would be nothing more than an amusing story he'd tell once in a while for the mere pleasure of hearing it.

At the Nelsons' home, Katrina took the last plate off the dish drainer and started drying it with one of Edith's white kitchen towels. "Next time you need to let me wash as well as dry."

The older woman shook her head. "I can still wash my own dishes. You're company here, you know."

"Well, when you put on a dinner like you did, someone else should do the dishes," Katrina said. "I haven't had real fried chicken like that since—well, I don't know if I've ever eaten any so good."

Edith beamed. "You should go take a rest when we finish up here. The boys are napping with Charley so your time's your own."

Katrina added a dried plate to the stack she was building. She didn't know where Edith kept her various dishes so the older woman was planning to put everything in the cupboard when they finished.

"I'd like to take another walk down to that heart sign," Katrina said as she folded her damp dish towel. "Maybe I can get some good pictures of it with no one around."

Katrina wanted some fresh air. Since she'd opened her heart again to God, she felt like she'd been hollowed out. Her emotions echoed around inside of herself and she wanted to have some time alone to at least identify them. She wasn't willing to use Conrad or her cancer as an excuse to stop her emotions again. She was going to live fully for however long she was able to take breath.

Edith nodded. "That stop sign is special to people around here. You know my daughter, Doris June, was the young girl in the pickup truck that hit the sign. Charley's son. I was so adamant she was too young to be eloping that she broke up with the young man. Each year that my daughter didn't marry after that, I felt guilty for ruining her life."

"But you didn't know," Katrina said.

"No more than you did with your parents," Edith agreed. "I'm just saying that regret and guilt can fester inside us until we are full of more darkness than light. None of us can tell the future. Or control what other people will do. All we can do is trust God with each of our own days."

Katrina reached over and gave the older woman a hug.

"I'll send word after I have the next cancer tests," she offered. "So you know what the doctor says."

"Thank you. I wanted to ask if you'd do that, but I didn't want to make you feel you had to give me the information," Edith said.

"Just don't tell Conrad," Katrina added. "Unless he asks."

Edith nodded.

"I don't want to disturb him if he's—" Katrina swallowed. "Moving on is the term people use."

Just then there was a knock at the front door.

Edith took off her apron and they both started walking out of the kitchen. Katrina recognized the visitor through the colored glass window on the front door and started walking faster.

"It's my sister," she said as she threw the door open. "Leanne," she cried out as she enveloped her sister in a hug. Then she stood back. "Let me look at you. How are you? Was it easy to find us? What's been happening?"

Katrina stood still and rejoiced at the sight of her sister. Leanne had short blond hair which she usually kept smoothly combed. Now it was in wild disarray. Her sister wasn't wearing her usual makeup, either. And her eyes had dark circles under them. She was wearing jeans and a red pullover.

"I stopped by the church and a man sent me over here. I think it was the pastor."

"You look a sight," Katrina said as she embraced her sister again. "Come inside. This is Edith."

The older woman nodded. "And you must be Leanne."

Leanne nodded and then burst into tears. "Oh, Katrina, what went wrong? I should have listened to you. You told me not to marry Walker in the first place. I should have listened."

"Shh," Katrina said gently as she pulled her sister to her and patted her on the shoulder. "Those things I said—I don't know the future today and I didn't back then. I certainly didn't know anything about

Walker that would have told you not to marry him. I was just worried about you living on the reservation."

"Walker's been withdrawn for months now and he snaps at the boys for no reason. I thought that was because he was discouraged about not finding work. Times are hard all over the reservation," Leanne said.

Katrina looked over her sister's head and met Edith's gaze.

"Do you and Walker still go to that little church you joined when you were dating?" Katrina asked. "Maybe the pastor there could talk with you and—"

"We stopped going about a year ago. Walker got mad at some of the people and said he wouldn't set foot inside the place again. I didn't want to go without him. It seemed disloyal and upset him, but I missed—"

Her sister started to cry even more and Katrina led her through the living room and into the dining room. "Why don't we sit down and rest a little? We saved a plate from dinner for you. Once you've eaten, things will look better. It'll be ready before long."

Katrina went into the kitchen, but Edith had already gotten there before her.

"I put the plate in the oven," the older woman said. "It wasn't even cold yet so it shouldn't take long. Why don't you take your sister a cup of tea?"

"I need to call the sheriff, too. He'll want to talk to her as soon as he can."

Edith nodded. "I'll take care of calling him. You make the tea. The kettle has hot water in it and the cups are in the cupboard to my right. You can either fill up a mug or use one of my good cups and saucers. The English ones are the best."

"Thanks. But I think mugs are best today. A cup and saucer shows every nervous bone in a person's hand. Leanne will want to be steady."

Katrina walked over to the cupboard indicated and pulled down a navy mug. She then poured hot water into the mug and reached up to the smaller cupboard where Edith kept her basket of wrapped tea bags.

With that, Katrina took the mug of hot water and the basket of teas out to the dining table. Leanne could sit there while she waited for her dinner to warm up. Edith had even saved a piece of blueberry pie for her.

Leanne had just finished her last bite of her chicken dinner when there was a knock on the front door. Edith had been sitting on the sofa in the living room, looking through a magazine, so she called out that she would get the door. Katrina wasn't surprised when she heard the voice of Sheriff Wall.

Edith brought the man into the dining room.

"Sorry to interrupt your dinner," the sheriff said as he twisted his Stetson in his hand. "I suppose you know about your husband reporting your car stolen?"

Leanne nodded. "It's not true."

"I figured as much by now," he said. "I'm hoping you don't mind me asking some questions."

"You better ask them before I go find the bed Edith promised me," Leanne said. "You might not see me for days once that happens."

The sheriff smiled slightly and brought out a small notebook from his pocket. "The first question is about timing. Could you tell me what happened yesterday? I'd like a general feel for things."

Leanne told the sheriff about how her husband had been staying out at night and not telling her where he'd been. She mentioned that he'd bought a couple of new shirts and she didn't know where he got the money. She said that she thought he must be having an affair.

"What else could I think?" she stopped to ask Edith and Katrina. "When my husband started coming home at daybreak and wearing a new shirt? I didn't even think he was trying to hide anything. If I didn't have the boys, I would have tried to follow him one night to see where he went."

"Did Walker ever hit you or threaten you?" the sheriff asked.

Leanne hesitated. "Saturday he said I should leave or I could be hurt bad. At first, I thought he meant *he'd* hurt me, but when I think about it now, sometimes I think he was warning me about someone else. That doesn't make sense, though. Who else would hurt me? I know he was mad about the gray car. He must have wanted to sell it. That's the only reason I can think of to explain why he was so angry that I lent it out to Katrina. I don't know if he'd get much for it, but it's the only asset we have that would even bring in a few hundred dollars. I don't know why he reported it stolen."

"Speaking of valuables," the sheriff said. "Your house was ransacked. Can you think of any reason why?"

Leanne shook her head. "We never claimed to have much. Walker did sometimes joke about his streets of gold, but everyone knew he was just talking. He even stopped saying that when we stopped going to church. There wasn't anyone else around who would think it was funny then anyway. We had no other friends."

The sheriff nodded and wrote down a couple of notes. "Maybe, if he was having an affair, it was the other woman who broke into your house. She might have been looking for something like pictures of the two of them together or—"

Leanne drew in her breath. "Surely Walker would never leave something like that around for the boys to find. He's not one of those terrible fathers. Do you really think another woman came into our house looking for something?"

The sheriff shrugged. "She could have been the one your husband was warning you about. Maybe she wasn't looking for something, but just wanted revenge."

"Oh, dear," Leanne said.

"These affairs can come to bad endings." The sheriff closed his notebook. "The other thing I need is to verify your identify. I suppose you have a driver's license with you?"

"Of course," Leanne said and she reached down to pick up the purse she'd set by her chair. She put the purse on the dining room table and pulled a wallet out of it. She opened the wallet and gave it to the sheriff. Her driver's license was clearly visible through a plastic sleeve.

The sheriff looked at the license and nodded. "Well, this is it then. Let me know if you want me to put in a request for a restraining order against your husband. I already have a request with the tribal authorities for them to let me know when he goes back home. I could add a request for protection."

"I think he'll be fine if he just cools off. And when I bring the car home, of course."

"You want to be sure it's safe before you go back there," Edith warned. "Give the sheriff some time to work. Katrina is planning to be here tomorrow to help photograph pictures for our church directory so the rest of you should stay at least that long, too."

"I'm sorry there have been problems about the car," Katrina said to her sister. "I should have just taken the Lexus and—"

It hit Katrina like a revelation. If she hadn't been driving the gray car, the muffler would never have fallen off. She wouldn't have driven down the road to this little town. She never would have met Edith and Charley. And, most important of all, she would never have sat beside Conrad on the steps of a small country church hearing the voice of a preacher and crying away all the anger she had inside.

One little thing could have changed her whole life. Then she looked back at her sister. That same little thing had changed Leanne's life, too.

"I don't want you to feel guilty," Leanne said as she reached over and put her hand on Katrina's arm. "Neither one of us knew this was going to be a problem with the car."

Katrina nodded. "Thank you for saying that."

Everyone was quiet for a minute and then Edith said, "You know, Sheriff, there's plenty of blueberry pie left, if you'd like a slice."

"That's the best offer I've had all day."

Katrina went out with the older woman to bring in the pie along with plates and forks for everyone.

"I'd love to get your recipe," Katrina said

as Edith started to cut the pie. "I'm thinking I could add food photography to the kinds of photos I'll try to sell. Your crust is beautiful."

Edith nodded. "Egg whites are the secret. Whip up one or two of them and coat the crust with them. It makes it brown better and look shiny. I'll show you someday. You can even take a picture of the pie before we eat it."

"That reminds me," the sheriff said as Edith slid him a slice of pie. "Barbara tells me we're signed up to have our photos taken at nine o'clock tomorrow morning for the church directory. She said the men are supposed to wear shirts with some color. I was wondering if I should wear my sheriff's uniform?"

"Do you have any solid color shirts besides white?" Katrina asked.

"I have a brown one." The sheriff took a bite of his pie and nodded his pleasure to Edith.

"Go ahead and wear your white one then," Katrina said. "I'm not sure we want to put your uniform in the directory."

"Folks all know I'm the sheriff anyway. And it's not like I'm advertising for more work."

Katrina chuckled. "I guess that's true. Still, white would be the one."

"That's what Barbara thought." The sheriff set his fork down and he was only halfway through with his pie. "She's home now ironing my shirt. Said she wants our family to look respectable." He looked around in bewilderment. "Now, you tell me, why does a sheriff have to wear a dress shirt to be respectable? The thing is—" The sheriff paused. "I'm thinking maybe I should wear my suit. The way Barbara is going to so much work for this picture reminds me that we never did get a wedding picture taken. We don't really have one of the two of us except for snapshots."

"A suit would be perfect then."

"What a lovely idea," Edith added.

"And maybe you could take our picture with us standing up front in the church. That's where we stood when we said our marriage vows."

"I have a rose bouquet Barbara could hold," Edith said. "The flowers are silk and would look real in a picture. I keep it just in case we have a bride who needs to borrow them."

Leanne sighed. "I just love a good wedding."

"It's not really a wedding." The sheriff looked panicked. "It's just a picture."

"If you at least said the vows, it would make the picture look more like a wedding one," Katrina added. "There's something about saying the words that gives people that glow on their faces."

"I could barely get the vows out the first time. My throat went dry and I had to cough and—"

"Barbara would probably really appreciate it if you did your vows again," Edith said. "That's a wonderful idea."

"I guess I could write them out," the sheriff said. "I'm just not very good at public speaking."

"Cake," Edith said. "We should have a little cake to go along with the vows."

Katrina wondered if the sheriff and his wife, Barbara, knew how fortunate they were. It wasn't about saying the vows or having a picture taken. The important thing is that they had decided to love each other through thick and thin, sickness and health. Katrina hadn't quite appreciated, until she had cancer, what an enormous gift it was to promise someone to stay with them when they were sick. Obviously, not every man was able to make that kind of a commitment.

Chapter Twelve

Conrad couldn't imagine that his aunt had really run out of sugar, but when she called up at seven o'clock in the morning and asked him to bring her a cup, he did the only thing he could and measured out some of the white stuff, put it in a plastic bag, and set out for her house. He hadn't slept at all last night and hadn't shaved this morning. But he wasn't going to explain that to his aunt, not when he was usually up and ready to go at six.

He didn't really need to walk past the church on the way to his aunt's house, but just to prove how fine he was, he decided to check and see if there was a backdrop for Katrina to use when she took her pictures for the directory. He was a gentleman. He knew she'd have trouble if she tried to line the people up against the door of the church. That old door had more scratches and scrapes than he could count.

He had an orange tarp in the garage that didn't have any grease stains and he'd thought about offering that but, even with his eyes feeling kind of dry and grainy, he could tell orange was a poor color for a background. Maybe when he dropped off the sugar to his aunt he would ask if she had any tablecloths that would look good draped over the door.

There was no doubt Katrina was going to need help. Herding people through their appointment times wouldn't be easy; he'd learned that when he'd had his grand opening a few months ago and offered to give free oil changes to the first fifty customers who came to his shop. He had to keep everyone moving or they got unruly. People around here tended to be outspoken.

He knew he didn't need to worry about Katrina, but he did anyway. As long as she was in this town, he seemed to be tangled up in being responsible for her. At first it was the report of the stolen car and now it was the church directory. He always believed in doing his civic duty and sometimes that was not convenient.

Conrad kept twisting that bag of sugar as he walked to his uncle's house. At least it didn't look like it would rain today. Everyone would take better pictures in the sunlight. He walked up to the back door of his uncle's house and knocked. Hopefully, Aunt Edith would be in the kitchen since she's the one who needed sugar.

The door was opened and Conrad was pulled into the kitchen before he had time to say his little speech about how he had to be leaving.

"Stir that," his aunt ordered him as she gave him a spoon and pointed at a boiling pot on the stove.

Conrad did what he was told. He did look around just to be sure his aunt was the only one in the kitchen. He relaxed when he saw that she was.

Then he noticed that she was beating something in a large ceramic bowl. She was wearing a flowered apron over an old housedress. And she had slippers on her feet as well as those pink wind-up curlers in her hair.

"What are you making?"

"Wedding cake," his aunt said and then turned to look at him. "Land's sake, what did you do to yourself?"

"I just woke up."

"Well," his aunt eyed him a bit longer, "you have a suit, don't you? Come to the church at nine o'clock."

Conrad stopped stirring. "I know Uncle Charley put that prayer request in the bulletin, but you can't just go and plan a wedding like this. People need to consent."

"Oh, it's not for you," his aunt said impatiently. "Other people might want to get married even if you don't."

"You don't mean Katrina?" he asked in astonishment. She'd never even looked at another man here. "It's that Pete, isn't it? I know he's a real charmer, but I didn't think Katrina would fall for his nonsense."

He realized he was stirring the pot a little fast, but who could blame him? He didn't like to see any woman taken advantage of that way.

"You're ruining my frosting base," Aunt Edith said as she walked over to the stove. "Here, let me. You go over and start cracking the eggs I have on the counter. Separate the whites and the yolks."

"I'm sorry. I guess I'm a little distracted."

"Is that what you call it?" his aunt asked and shook her head. "For your information, the wedding is for the sheriff. He and Barbara are restating their wedding vows before they get their photo taken this morning."

"Oh," Conrad said. "Well, why didn't you say so?"

"I just did. I thought he might like a best man," his aunt said. "He seems a little nervous so you might have to talk him through it."

"Nervous? He's already married."

"When you finish with those eggs," his aunt continued, "I need you to get the bouquet down. It's on the top shelf in the closet of your old room. The one the boys are in. And then go home and get your suit ready."

Conrad frowned. "Is the sheriff wearing a suit? No wonder he's jittery. If he wears his uniform, I should just wear mine from the station."

"This is a wedding," his aunt said as she lifted her head from her stirring and looked at him. "You need to dress like it."

"Yes, ma'am."

Conrad stood there cracking eggs with his thumb. It probably wasn't the best of times to wonder if all his life would be spent worrying about other people's doings instead of his own. He was poised to take some great leap, but he didn't have the courage to go over the edge. Still, even though he might not feel life as intensely as others, he wouldn't be crushed by grief, either. He just had to get through today. Katrina would probably be leaving tomorrow. The next day at the latest. He'd survive.

Katrina hurried to get dressed. She thought she had set her alarm for seven o'clock, but it hadn't gone off. Now she was late in helping Edith make the cake for the sheriff and she didn't have time to get everything ready for the pictures she'd be taking, either. She ran the comb through her hair and straightened the ivory top she'd worn with her jeans for the third day now. She'd have to go back to Leanne's house soon for her suitcase if nothing else.

The sunlight was streaming in through the windows as she went down the stairs. Leanne and the boys were sleeping in late. Katrina didn't expect to see them before noon.

"I'm sorry I'm late," she said when she turned into the dining room. She could see

Edith standing at the stove. "The alarm didn't go off and—"

She stepped into the kitchen and saw Conrad standing there with an egg on his thumb.

"Oh," she said as she stopped.

"Aunt Edith needed some sugar," he said stiffly. "And I wanted to ask about her tablecloths anyway. I thought you might need a backdrop for your photos."

"For the pictures! Of course, I don't know why I didn't think of that," Katrina said. "For outside photos I generally use a leafy tree or a wall of ivy or a riverbank."

There was a moment's silence.

"In a month we'd have leaves on the trees," Edith said. "But for now, people will just need to stand in front of the church."

Katrina winced. "That might not look very good. For one thing, if people stand on the ground, the basement lifts the church up by four feet so half of the photo would be concrete and the line between the concrete and the actual building would be too dominant for the pictures. Everyone would look like they're cut in half. And at the top of the stairs, those old doors are scuffed pretty bad."

"I do have a couple of lace tablecloths," Edith said thoughtfully. "One of them in particular is quite nice. And then, of course, I have my fruit tablecloths. They're colorful."

"You don't happen to have a nice solid blue tablecloth, do you?"

Edith shook her head. "I might have a sheet that's blue, though."

"Why don't we just gather up a few things and take them over with us?" Katrina said. "That way we'll have some options for people. They can be inside the church or outside."

"I have some plastic fruit that goes with my fruit tablecloths," Edith said. "You know pears, apples, bananas and a few grapes."

"Yesterday some of the old men asked if they could have their pictures taken with their guns," Conrad said. "Or their dogs."

"I'm going to make a firm rule that no one holds anything," Katrina said.

"I told them I didn't think it would work. So we'll see how they show up. One insisted he could at least wear a hunting vest. Something about the freedom of speech and how the church directory committee shouldn't dictate to people."

Edith exclaimed, "That's what we needed! A committee. Why didn't we think of that?"

Katrina shrugged. "It's too late now. How can I help with this cake anyway?"

"Here," Conrad said. "You can finish the eggs. Then I can go bring the tablecloths out for everyone to look at."

An hour and a half later, Katrina and Edith were getting ready to carry the cake over to the church. Charley had decided to stay home with the boys. Conrad had left earlier to go back to his house and change into a suit.

"He managed to bring Leanne's car back," Katrina said as she opened the front door and stepped out on the street. The gray car stood at the curb with freshly washed windows. Conrad must have brought the car around before he went home to change.

"Conrad is very prompt in getting his vehicles back to folks," Edith said. "He knows people need transportation around here."

"I suppose he left the keys on the dining room table?" Katrina asked.

Edith nodded. "I saw them when I walked through to get my coat."

"Well, I hope he left his bill, too." Katrina

didn't want any favors from the man. She was going to say that he hoped he charged his full prices, too, when Edith spoke.

"I wish I had a dress that fit you," the older woman said to Katrina.

"What I have is fine," Katrina said, grateful for the interruption in her thoughts. She didn't need to drag Edith into her feelings about Conrad. "I'm just the eyes behind the camera. Besides I have to carry this bag anyway so the neckline on a dress would pull this way or that way and it would look funny."

"Still, a wedding is a festive occasion. We haven't had one all winter so I'm kind of looking forward to it."

"I'm glad Conrad called and juggled the appointments so we have a full half hour to spend with the sheriff and his wife."

"Isn't this the sheriff's car right here?" Edith said as they walked close to the steps of the church. "He's parked right in front. I wonder if we should put a 'Just Married' sign on his car for when they pull away."

"I think we'll have enough to do with the cake and the pictures," Katrina said as she held out her hand to take the cake from Edith. "Why don't you go up the stairs first. I'll follow with the cake."

"I hope Conrad is here," Edith said as she made her way up the stairs.

Katrina didn't comment. She was hoping he'd stay for the wedding and then leave. How was she supposed to concentrate and take pictures with him around?

The cake Katrina was holding was white with lemon filling and a vanilla frosting. It was an eight-inch triple layer cake so it stood tall in its carrier. Edith fretted about not having a wedding couple to put on top of the cake so she brought out two of the gingerbread men they'd made and formed a bonnet for one of them.

Katrina followed Edith into the church and stopped to look around. She hadn't been inside a church for twenty years. This church even smelled the same as the one in her childhood. It must be the lemon polish on the wooden pews. These pews were not new, but they shone. The sunlight came in a slant through the stained glass windows. The pattern in the windows was not elaborate; it was just a flower with a stem and a leaf. Perhaps it was a rose.

And then Katrina saw the three people at the front of the church. The sheriff and Conrad were talking. A woman, it must be

Barbara, had turned and was walking down the aisle toward them. She had on a street-length white lace dress.

"I wore what we got married in," the dark-haired woman said to Edith. "Remember?"

"Of course, I do," Edith said and turned slightly. "You know our new friend, Katrina? She's the one who's going to take your picture."

Barbara smiled and held out her hand. "Carl mentioned you."

It took Katrina a moment to remember that Carl was the sheriff's first name.

"Here, let me set this down," Katrina said as she laid the cake carrier on one of the pew benches so she could shake hands.

As soon as the two women had greeted each other, the noise from the front of the church grew louder. Katrina couldn't hear what the sheriff and Conrad were saying, but she could see they were arguing. And at a wedding.

Conrad saw the women look down the aisle at him so he lowered his voice to speak with the sheriff. "You can't have someone say your vows for you. This is a wedding."

"Well, it's not official," Sheriff Wall said. "Neither one of us are free to marry."

"That's because you're married to each other!"

"Besides," the man continued. "I'm not asking you to say them for me really. You'd be more like a teleprompter. You say the words and I repeat them."

Conrad shook his head. "I might not know much about women, but I don't think Barbara would like that. Your vows are supposed to be from your heart, not from the heart of someone standing next to you."

"I never was much good at public speaking." The sheriff shook his head.

"Well, you got through your wedding the first time."

"I was desperate then. I'd have done anything to marry Barbara."

"Well, you shouldn't have volunteered to do it again then."

"I didn't so much volunteer as get drafted," the sheriff said. "My idea was to just take the picture like we'd said our vows. It was your aunt's idea to make it real."

"Ah," Conrad said. "My aunt does like a wedding."

The sheriff ran his finger around his shirt

collar. He wore a white shirt with a brown suit jacket and a plain brown tie.

"Here they come," the sheriff said.

"Just keep thinking about the cake you'll get when it's all over," Conrad said. "I've heard it said that if you want to look smitten about someone think about food."

"I like cake," the sheriff said hopefully.

By that time the bride and her escorts had arrived at the front of the church.

Katrina set her bag down on the nearest pew and pulled her camera out. "Now, if everyone will just take their places. I'll be taking pictures at various times as you say your vows."

She arranged the couple with Conrad standing behind them the way a best man should.

"And stand in the sunlight. You're looking a little pale," she added with a look at the sheriff. "Now there's no one here so go ahead and say your vows to each other. I'll be walking around getting shots from various angles."

Katrina started looking through her camera lens, but it was silent so she looked back up again.

"Who's going to go first?" she asked.

"Ladies first," the sheriff said.

Barbara blushed and Katrina went back to looking through her lens. She hardly listened to the words the woman was saying. However, she could see the love on Barbara's face and Katrina got some great shots of her looking at the sheriff.

"Okay," Katrina said after it had been silent for a minute or so. "It's your turn, Sheriff."

Katrina kept her eye looking through the camera lens.

The sheriff swallowed. Then he cleared his throat. Then he ran his finger around the neck of his shirt.

Then Barbara's face crumbled. "You can't say your vows!"

"Yes, yes, I can," the sheriff said. "I just need a minute to gather my thoughts when I see how beautiful you are."

That made his wife smile again. "You look pretty good yourself."

"Marrying you was the best thing I ever did," the sheriff said, his voice soft and intimate.

Katrina took a picture of them gazing into each other's eyes. And one of them kissing. Neither Barbara nor the sheriff looked like models. The sheriff had a line on his forehead that showed where his hat set. Barbara's face was fuller than it should be. But they had the kind of heart the calendar people would love.

Katrina was so surprised, she almost stopped taking photos. She realized she'd done nothing to bring the emotion out in these photos. The feelings were there because of what was in the couple's heart. Maybe she had gone about her photos all wrong. Instead of trying to create scenes that looked believable she should have found the people who genuinely felt the emotions.

She moved the lens slightly and saw Conrad. The emotion on his face was just as strong as on the sheriff's. Only he looked miserable.

Just then a cell phone rang and she looked up from her camera. The sheriff reached into his pocket and pulled out his phone. "Sheriff Wall here."

He listened for a few minutes and then hung up.

"Where's your sister?" he turned to ask Katrina.

"At Edith's house, sleeping. Along with the boys. I think Charley's there, too. Why?"

"That was the tribal authorities. Walker

must have gone back to the house last night. They found him this morning beaten up pretty bad. They are sending him to Billings General Hospital. He kept trying to tell them something about Dry Creek so he must have figured out where Leanne and the boys are."

"Will he be all right?" Katrina asked.

The sheriff nodded. "They thought so. They just want to figure out what is going on at that house." He paused. "Your sister was here all night, wasn't she?"

"Of course," Katrina snapped back. "Besides, she couldn't beat up Walker if she wanted to."

"I guess that's true. Someone's out to hurt that family, though."

"Leanne and the boys need to stay away from the reservation until they find out what's happening," Katrina agreed. "They can come back to Los Angeles with me if they need for a while."

"They can stay at my place, too," Edith offered. "Surely the authorities will find out more about it all when Walker is able to talk to them."

"We hope so." The sheriff reached for his hat.

"Should I have Leanne call you? Or I can walk over to the house and get her now," Katrina said. "Even with all the trouble, I know she'll want to go to the hospital and see Walker."

The sheriff nodded. "She can wait to call until she gets back from the hospital. If she's been here all the time since I talked to her last, she obviously doesn't know anything about who would have broken into their house anyway."

"Thanks," Katrina said.

"I can walk over with you," Conrad offered as she put her camera back in the bag.

She looked up at him. He was the man who had given her tissues every time she cried lately. He'd offered her a job when he thought she needed one. He'd brought her to church and he'd held her hand. But it wasn't enough. Not after she'd seen the love shining in the faces of Barbara and the sheriff. She didn't want to be with someone who was afraid to love her.

"No, thanks," Katrina said softly. "I'm fine on my own. I better see a bill for that new muffler you put on Leanne's car, too."

With that, she turned and walked out of the church.

Chapter Thirteen

Katrina slid her camera down the table slightly so she could see her sister better. They were both in Edith's dining room. Katrina had given all the information she had to Leanne and her sister had called the hospital in Billings to learn that Walker would be sedated until mid-afternoon because they were operating on his leg.

Leanne insisted Katrina return to the church and finish taking the photos. "These people have been so kind to us. We need to do what we can to repay them. Besides, Walker doesn't need either of us right now."

"He may later." Katrina might not care about Walker's pain, but she did care if her sister was in distress. She didn't want to leave her alone to face this.

"Or maybe he needs the woman he's been sneaking off to visit," Leanne said, hurt and anger lacing her voice. "Maybe he wants her to visit."

"You don't know that he's—" Katrina tried. She'd misjudged so much in her life, she didn't want to add any more misunderstandings to the list, but she couldn't give her sister false hope, either.

"I just don't know how else to explain what's happening." Leanne's lips trembled slightly. "I'd never seen him like the way he was the other day. Something is very wrong."

"Still, until you know—"

Leanne turned so she faced her squarely. "You're sweet to worry, but right now, I'm going to make breakfast for the boys and Charley. Then I'll call the hospital again and see when Walker can have visitors. By then, maybe I'll know what to do."

Katrina reached out and touched her sister's shoulder. She hadn't noticed Leanne was so frail until she felt her bones. "It's okay if you need to talk about it. I know there's a lot in our past that we didn't discuss—that I couldn't find the words to say—but I want a better relationship for us from now on."

"Me, too." Leanne reached over and enclosed the hand Katrina had on her shoulder. "You're my older sister and I've missed you. That's why I wanted you to come visit."

"If you want me to go with you to the hospital to see Walker, just let me know."

Katrina almost added she'd had lots of experience with hospitals, but then stopped herself. She couldn't tell Leanne about the cancer today. Not with all she faced regarding Walker.

Leanne smiled a little. "You know, it's almost a relief to know there's something behind his absences even if I don't know what—or who—it is. At least, I know I'm not going crazy."

"Maybe he has a gambling problem and it has nothing to do with another woman," Katrina suggested.

Leanne laughed. "Go take the photos. You know Walker and I don't have enough money to get into a gambling problem."

Katrina stood up and gave her sister another quick hug. She had hope for a relationship with Leanne again and that's something she hadn't had for a long time. "Come over when you're finished with breakfast. I'd like to take a few shots of you and the boys. They'll want their quarters."

"Quarters?"

"It's an aunt/nephew thing," Katrina said as she put her camera bag over her shoulder and started toward the door. The last thing she wanted to do was disappoint her nephews.

As she stepped out into the open air, she looked at her watch. If she hurried, she would be ready for her nine-thirty appointments.

The wind was blowing, and it looked like rain. That garden gnome would have to stand there without her paying any attention to him. When she'd left, people were starting to come to the church and Katrina knew she'd have to sort out who went first. If she didn't take pictures in the order of the appointments, she wouldn't know if she had missed someone. One thing was clear, though. There would be no outside pictures, not unless the weather got better.

She was surprised when she stepped back inside the church sanctuary to find that everyone was lined up. Conrad was standing at the head of the line with a clipboard. Edith and Barbara were passing out small pieces of cake on paper plates and everyone was talking and eating and having a good time.

Everyone, that is, except for Conrad. He looked harried. She should have known he'd do his duty until the bitter end.

"Any man who needs a blue shirt, raise your hand," Conrad called out, trying to make himself heard over the chatter. He didn't know what had made him come back here, but he couldn't leave Katrina to face this crowd by herself. "Elmer has a couple of shirts that can go out on loan. One snap, two buttoned. Remember, this is for the church. We want to look our best."

"Can I hold my football trophy in my picture?" an old man asked. He had a large leather bag in his hands and he was holding it close to his chest like it contained pure gold.

"You never played a game of football in your life, Mr. Dailey, and you know it," Conrad said. "So who'd you get the trophy from? Your grandson?"

"So what if I did," the man said, sticking his chin out. "It's all in the family. If it wasn't for me, he wouldn't be alive to win that trophy."

"The rules say no one gets anything extra

in their photo," Conrad said as he held out his hand for the bag.

"Harry Bliss gets to keep his toupee," one of the men called out. "Give the old man his trophy."

"Yeah, my face looks better with me holding a football trophy," Mr. Dailey agreed as he put the bag behind his back as if hiding it would make Conrad forget all about it. "Besides, some of those women in Miles City like an athletic man. We are going to send the directory to Miles City, aren't we? They've got some good-looking widows up there."

Conrad ran his hands through his hair before turning back to the old man. Why did everything have to be so difficult? "Again, these pictures are for the church, not a dating service."

"Well, the church is where you got your wife," Mr. Dailey said indignantly. "If you're entitled to get help from the church, I'm entitled to help, too."

The whole building hushed. People's hands stopped with their plastic forks raised halfway to their mouths. One man paused in putting on a blue shirt. Conrad could feel everyone turning and looking at him.

"You know, the prayer bulletin," Mr. Dailey added.

"I know about the prayer bulletin," Conrad snapped back. "And, for the record, that prayer bulletin should be kept for serious business and not some romantic nonsense. And, it didn't work anyway."

The silence in the church was because of shock. Conrad knew he only had a few seconds before the protest broke through. He had made a mistake, he just didn't know how to fix it. He'd attacked romance and the prayer bulletin. Especially because he looked down the aisle and saw Katrina. He had been afraid she wouldn't come back after talking to her sister. And now he was wishing she hadn't.

"Look here, Conrad Nelson," Tracy said. "Romance is not nonsense. And that prayer bulletin did so work. Katrina's here, isn't she? Just because you and Pete have some bachelor thing going, doesn't mean there aren't nice men around here who would like to marry a woman like me or Katrina."

Conrad heard Katrina's grunt of surprise even from where he was standing.

"And," Tracy continued as she put her

hands on her hips. She didn't let Katrina's shock stop her. "Those men are willing to put some romance into making that happen. They don't just pray about it and then not do anything."

At that, Tracy turned to give him a stern look.

"There are things that—" Conrad began. "I'm just saying there are things you don't know."

Conrad looked around at everyone until his eyes came to Katrina. His gaze caught her eyes and held them. "You're right. I'm sure there are hundreds of men who would be willing to romance women like the two of you."

"Well," Tracy said, sounding satisfied now that she'd made her point.

Katrina just looked at him for a minute. Then she looked away. "Well, everyone line up. Who's next to get their picture taken?"

Conrad looked away, too. He'd lost her. He didn't know if God had answered anyone's prayers by bringing his calendar woman to Dry Creek. He might have become a little infatuated with the woman in the picture, but it was Katrina he'd miss. He already felt the hollowness inside.

* * *

Katrina walked down the middle of the aisle to the front of the church. People parted to let her through. She was all business now. She wanted to get these pictures taken so she could leave. She didn't know what the old man had meant by the prayer bulletin, but she knew what Tracy meant and she agreed. There was no point chasing after a man who wasn't ready to make a commitment.

"I'm next," Tracy said when Katrina reached the front.

"Good." Katrina set her camera bag down on the closest pew and took out what she needed to take pictures.

"Is your sister all right?" Tracy asked while Katrina decided what angle she wanted to shoot from. "Edith told me what was happening."

"Thanks. I think she'll be fine." Katrina looked around the church sanctuary. "Now, where would you like your picture taken?"

"Probably just one of the walls around here." Tracy looked at the two side walls. "I guess they all need painting. But then I probably do, too."

"Nonsense," Katrina said as she searched

for a place on the side wall that would be long enough to use as a backdrop. "You're a beautiful woman." She shot a look over at Conrad. "Some men just don't appreciate strong women."

"Oh, Conrad's okay," Tracy said sheepishly. "He just got what I should have said to Pete."

Katrina didn't agree, but she wasn't going to inform Tracy of the man's faults. Instead, she found what she was looking for and motioned the other woman over. "To your left between those two windows."

Tracy walked over and stood in the spot. She fluffed up her hair and brushed any lint off her shoulders. Then her lips pressed together for a moment. "Speaking of Pete, I wanted to apologize for yesterday. I should have just let him meet with you alone. We're like oil and water."

Katrina nodded as she started to snap some photos of Tracy. "It's not a problem. I don't plan to use the few pictures I took of the two of you anyway. But—" she looked up from the camera "—for what it's worth, I think he has considerable affection for you."

A wistful smile lit up Tracy's face. Instinctively, Katrina lifted the camera to her eye and captured some haunting photos of Tracy's face. Love and despair battled in her expression.

After the last click, Tracy stood up and smoothed down her dress. Then she said, "It's not really his fault, you know."

"How can you say that?" Katrina asked, putting down her camera. She kept her voice low so no one else would hear. "He clearly has feelings for you and he won't do anything about it."

"He thinks I'm responsible for his younger brother's death," Tracy said softly as her face twisted. "And, some days, I'm not sure whether he's right or wrong."

With that, Tracy walked down the aisle and out of the church. Speechless, Katrina watched her go.

"I'm next," one of the older men said as he walked down the aisle of the church. He was clutching some of the fruit Edith had brought over and a book. "Richard Compton."

"Well, Mr. Compton, you know the rule. No extras. Besides, that fruit's artificial," Katrina said as he got closer. She was tired of being caught up in everyone's problems so she was glad to have one that was easy to solve.

"I'm not going to eat it," he protested. "I'm just using it to open up my negotiations. I'll give up the fruit if you let me hold a picture instead."

"What picture?" Katrina asked suspiciously.

Mr. Compton opened the book and took out a large old black-and-white photo of a young woman. She was wearing a black dress that was too big for her and had her hair scraped back in a bun. But her smile was soft with some deep affection for whoever stood next to that old camera. "This is my Ella. She's been gone for ten years now, but I still miss her. This is what she looked like when I first met her almost sixty-five years ago."

He held the photo to his chest. "I'd like folks to remember Ella, too, when they see my picture in the directory."

Katrina looked through her lens and took the shot. The look on the old man's face practically took her breath away. She took a few more shots and then lifted her eye from the lens so she could blink.

She'd never seen anything so beautiful. Everyone in the church was silent as they looked at the man and his Ella.

"I remember her," Edith finally said softly from where she stood to the side. "She was a remarkable woman."

"She brought me chicken soup once when I was sick," someone else said. "The best soup I ever ate."

"My mom still talks about her," a young woman said.

Katrina had to blink a couple of more times. And then, just when she needed a tissue, Conrad was there with a folded handkerchief.

"Here," he said as he held it out to her.

"I don't need—" Katrina started to say when a tear rolled down her cheeks. She reached over and took the handkerchief. "Thanks."

"My pleasure," he said.

And then he just stood and looked at her like that old man had looked at his Ella. It all made Katrina want to cry even more. She needed to remind herself that he wasn't going to do anything about his feelings. He was a disciplined man and he knew what he wanted and didn't want in his life.

"I'm ready for the next person," Katrina said as she took one final swipe at her tears. She'd leave as soon as she got the pictures all taken. Maybe she could follow Leanne into Billings to visit Walker at the hospital. Then she could stay in a hotel for a night or two until her sister was ready to go home. She needed to leave Dry Creek.

Chapter Fourteen

Conrad sat on the church steps. The sun was beginning to set and the last photo had been taken. No one needed his clipboard anymore. Katrina had taken her final shot and walked back to his aunt's house. He should feel good that he'd done all he could to get the church directory pictures taken in an orderly fashion. Instead, he felt like he'd been run over by a tractor with studded tires.

He looked down the street to where his shop stood. It didn't even bother him that he'd been closed for the day. He was a coward and it was killing him. He didn't need Tracy to tell him that he'd failed at love in some major way. He'd expected the churn of emotions inside him to ease up when he knew he couldn't go any further with Katrina, but they didn't.

For the first time in his life, he began to wonder if his father would have chosen to marry his mother even if he'd known she would die too soon. He wished he'd thought to ask him the question on one of his father's more lucid days when he talked about the good times they'd had as a family before his mother passed away.

Uncle Charley had been his father's brother. He wondered if the two men had ever talked about Conrad's mother's death. He wasn't quite sure why, but the question seemed to him suddenly to be very important to ask.

He reached in his pocket to pull out his cell phone when he realized he didn't have the phone with him. He must have left it in his shop when he came back over here the last time. Not that it mattered, he'd just stop in the hardware store on his way back to his shop and ask his uncle then. As he walked down the asphalt road, he noticed a tiny green blade of grass breaking through the ground. It wouldn't be long now until spring was fully in bloom. He took the blade as a sign of hope as he quickened his steps. Maybe he could risk more than he thought.

The town was quiet after all of the coming and going for the church directory. A pickup he didn't recognize was parked across the street from his shop. If he wasn't in such a hurry, he'd check it out. It probably just belonged to a new cowboy out at the Elkton Ranch, though. They were supposed to be hiring a few more hands.

Conrad heard the lively discussion going on in the hardware store before he even stepped up to the porch. The door was open, probably because of the mild temperatures. He recognized his uncle Charley's voice before he set foot inside the building.

Shadows were beginning to gather in the corners of the store. The men were seated in wood chairs that circled the black potbelly stove even though there was no fire going today. It was the conversation and not the warmth the men came for anyway. Some of the store's chairs were missing spokes and some of them had chipped paint or scratches. But they were all assigned for life to the regulars that came here. Usually, a man sent word if he was going to miss a day by the stove so that the others would know the chair was open for a visitor.

"Uncle Charley," Conrad said by way of announcing his presence. He hadn't lived in Dry Creek long enough to be anything but a visitor here.

All six of the men sitting looked up at him.

"Hey, son," his uncle greeted him and, to his relief, got up and walked toward the door. "Coming over for a game of checkers?"

"Not today," Conrad said, stepping a little closer to his uncle so no one else would hear their conversation. "I just wondered if you could tell me something about my father."

Uncle Charley brightened. "Sure. Anything."

Conrad took a deep breath. "Did he ever regret marrying my mother? After she died, I mean. Did he wish he'd married someone else?"

"There was no one else for your father, not before or after. He loved your mother and that was it."

"I see."

"I've been trying to tell you there are no guarantees of any kind in life," his uncle continued gently. "We need to be happy when we find love and not worry so much about whether it will last forever. God only gives us one day at a time. The rest is in His hands."

Just then Elmer shouted, "Hey, what are they doing?"

The older man had been standing by the window of the hardware store, looking out over the street that went through Dry Creek. Now, he was pointing at something and sputtering. "Call the sheriff."

Conrad rushed over to the window. The sheriff was probably home by now and it would take him time to get back. "What's wrong?"

He only had to look down the street to see there were strange men in town. At that same moment, it occurred to him that the pickup he saw was too clean to have come from the Elkton Ranch. There was no dust on it. It had come in from the freeway. He should have followed his instinct and gone to check it out.

He strained to see what was happening. The men—two of them—were down by his uncle's house, standing on the street by the white fence. They were struggling with something that looked like his aunt's fruity tablecloth only it had legs and black strappy high heels.

"They've got Conrad's bride!" Elmer shouted out at the same time that Conrad realized they had Katrina wrapped up in that old tablecloth and, what with all the flapping around, it looked like they were trying to get her to go inside her sister's old gray car.

Conrad raced for the door.

"Wait," his uncle called him back. "You can't go out there with nothing in your hands."

And, with that, his uncle reached over to a shelf and threw him a brand-new shovel.

"Thanks," Conrad said as he opened the door and stepped onto the porch.

Katrina was mad. She was also a little scared, but she'd had a hard day and she didn't appreciate having a tablecloth thrown over her and scrawny arms trying to push her around. She'd been taking the tablecloth out to hang on the clothesline to freshen it up after using it all day for a backdrop for photos, when someone grabbed her.

She elbowed one of the attackers in his stomach and got a grunt for her efforts. "Let me go!"

"Shut up," one of them muttered and

she stomped on his foot with the heel of her shoes.

"Witch," he screamed. "You're going to be sorry."

Katrina tried to duck out of their arms, but the other man had a firm grip on her waist.

The man she had kicked started pressing her head down for some reason when she heard footsteps coming to her rescue.

"Let her go," Conrad shouted. She knew it was him by the sound of his voice.

"Call the sheriff," Katrina yelled.

There, she thought, that was the way things were done in civilized places. The authorities came and rescued people from kidnappers. Although why these two were interested in kidnapping her she had no idea.

"Nobody's calling the law," the man holding her waist said. She knew it was him because she'd been trying to twist free and he yelled in her ear. "Kyle, show them."

No sooner had the thought surfaced that having a name put her in a better negotiating position than she heard a blast.

"That was a gun," she said.

"No kidding," the other one, who must be Kyle, said with a sneer. She couldn't see his face to know he was sneering, but she figured he was.

"If you shot someone, you'll be sorry."

The man at her waist just laughed.

"No one's hurt," Conrad called out. Which relieved her until she realized he sounded closer. What was wrong with the man? He was supposed to be running off to get the sheriff. She knew Conrad did his duty, but he needed to use some sense.

She heard one footstep coming closer and the click of the gun. That did it. She took a deep breath, put her elbow into the stomach of the man holding her and stomped her foot again on Kyle.

She heard a howl and a grunt, but no gunshot so she felt good.

"What—are you nuts?" Kyle demanded when he stopped jumping around. "That old car ain't worth it."

She went still. "Which car?"

She found a tear in the cloth. Edith had said the tablecloth was old, but it had been whole until these guys decided to use it as a net. Mentally giving an apology to Edith, she straightened and put her nose in the opening. She shook her head back and forth until she made the hole bigger and could get half her head through the opening.

What she saw then made chills run down her back. Conrad was standing there with a shovel in his hands, daring those two degenerates to charge at him.

"You can have the car," she announced. Her sister had said it was only worth a couple of hundred dollars and she still had that in savings. She'd buy the thing if Leanne's husband was so wild to sell it.

"You don't need to give them anything," Conrad said.

"We need the key," Kyle said. He was a stocky, dark-haired man with a red bandanna tied around his forehead. At least he wasn't waving the gun around anymore. He had it pointed to the ground as he turned to talk to her.

The other man looked like a used car salesman. He had his hair slicked back with some kind of gel and a gold tooth in the front of his mouth. His brown T-shirt had a dirt bike pictured on it.

Katrina decided that neither one of her attackers looked too bright. Not that she was probably looking her best after pushing her head through a hole, either. "I don't have the key with me. What's wrong with you? I was just going out to the clothesline. You could see I didn't even have my purse."

She wanted to look around and see where everyone was standing, but she didn't want to alert her would-be captors that people were no doubt looking out of every window in town now that they'd fired that gun. She'd keep talking so they didn't think of that, either. She didn't want them shooting any more bullets around. The sheriff would be here before she knew it.

"Don't you have a pocket?" Kyle asked. "What do you have in your pocket?"

"Take the tablecloth away and I'll empty my pockets for you," she promised. "You'll see there's nothing in them but a tissue or two."

Conrad thought his heart was going to burst. Katrina kept talking to these thugs like she was at a garden party. If one of them would step away from her, he'd have a chance of bringing the man down with the side of the shovel. But he couldn't risk hitting her, not when she was standing so close, and now she was letting that man search the pockets on her jeans.

Please, God, help me, he thought. *I'd rather die myself than see this exasperating woman hurt.*

"I'll go get the key," Conrad offered. Didn't she know these men were dangerous?

"How do you know where it is?" Kyle lifted his head and asked suspiciously. All he'd brought out of Katrina's pocket was a soggy tissue and he didn't look too happy about it.

"Good point," Conrad said. "Maybe you should take me as your hostage and let her go get the key. She'll know where it is better than me. It's where it was this morning."

"Why would you do something like that?" Kyle frowned like he was trying to figure out what the catch was. "We could hurt you something fierce if she doesn't come back."

"He feels responsible for the whole world," Katrina muttered.

"Oh." Kyle tried to figure that out.

"Look," Conrad said, spreading his hands and setting the shovel down at his feet. "I'll cooperate. Let her go get the key."

The guy with the dirt bike on his shirt grunted. "Let her do it, Kyle. We can't stand here all day if she doesn't have it. Our orders were to get the stuff and get out of here."

"Well, Katrina is the one to get the key then," Conrad said with as much cheerful force as he could manage. These men would run around in circles if no one took charge of them. "Kyle, you let go and Mr.—" Conrad looked at the man "—Mr. Dirt Bike here you take my arm at the same time and we'll make the switch."

"I guess," Kyle said.

The Dirt Bike man was already reaching for him so Conrad cooperated by stepping closer. For a moment, he was near enough to Katrina to smell her perfume. If they got out of this alive, he was never going to let her go. Of course, now might not be the best time to tell her that. Not when she was looking at him like he was crazy.

"These men aren't playing around," she hissed at him.

"I know." The grip Dirt Bike man had on him would have told him that if he didn't already know it.

"You could get killed just being responsible, you know. The world doesn't need you to ride to its rescue all the time." Her eyes flashed and her chin got that stubborn look he'd come to recognize with affection.

He smiled at her. "Just go get the key,"

and then, because he couldn't help it, he added, "dear."

That apparently rendered her speechless, but at least she started walking back toward the kitchen.

"And don't get anything else. Just the key," he called after her. He suddenly worried she'd come out with one of Aunt Edith's butcher knives or that old ice pick his uncle kept. Conrad didn't want to say anything to warn Katrina, though, not with the men here listening to every word he had to say. "Ask Aunt Edith about it if you need."

Maybe his aunt would have sense enough to make Katrina stay inside. The sheriff had surely been called and would be driving into town any minute now.

"Dear, huh?" Dirt Bike man said with a smirk as he looked at Conrad. "So you're not out to rescue the whole world. It was just her."

"You got a problem with that?" Conrad twisted to look the man in the eye.

"No, no problem," the other man said with a chuckle. "Just passing the time, that's all."

Conrad watched as Katrina stepped into the house. Then he took a look around the town he'd come to love. He couldn't see all of it because Kyle had decided to help Dirt Bike man keep him in place. Conrad would have told them that they could ease up their muscles a little. Until he knew Katrina wasn't going to come back out here, he wasn't going anywhere.

He pondered a little on what it was that made a man love a woman.

"You ever have a girlfriend?" he asked Dirt Bike man because his face was the closest.

"Yeah," the man looked over in surprise. "Once."

Conrad could see in the man's eyes that he'd be standing right where Conrad was now if the situation had been reversed and his girl was in danger. "What happened?"

Dirt Bike man shrugged. "You know."

Conrad nodded. Strangely enough he did know. A man could love with all his heart, but that didn't guarantee him a happily ever after.

"Still, it was good to love her, right?" Conrad worried he might sound like some broken-hearted country western song, but Dirt Bike man finally nodded.

In the distance, Conrad heard a car. There was no siren, but he knew by the speed of its approach that it had to be Sheriff Wall.

"Did I mention that car you're stealing has a new muffler on it?" Conrad said in hopes his voice would distract the two men enough to make some difference to the sheriff. "The best one money could buy, too."

Then Conrad heard the sound of a helicopter coming and he smiled. The sheriff had decided to forget about the budget and get some reinforcements. He'd have to remember to vote for the man in the next election.

"What's that?" Kyle asked as he looked around. Fortunately, he didn't look overhead.

Dirt Bike man did, though, and he hit the ground.

"Under the car," he yelled to his partner. "They're coming at us from the sky."

Conrad decided now was the time to jump over his aunt's fence and run for the kitchen. His two captors didn't even seem to notice, not being huddled as they were under that old gray car.

The kitchen door was open when he got there and hands pulled him inside.

"What did you think you were doing?" Katrina scolded him before anyone else could even talk.

There was really only one answer to that

so he leaned in to kiss her. But she pulled back before he even got close and burst into tears. Then she ran out of the room.

"She's just upset," his aunt said as she stepped close and patted him on the shoulder. "She'll come around."

He nodded, but not because he agreed.

Conrad figured the only one around who might understand what had happened was Dirt Bike and he was busy at the moment. Just because a man loved a woman was no guarantee she'd love him back or even believe his feelings were real. He'd lost Katrina. He'd hesitated too long and it was over.

He walked out of the kitchen and saw that night was coming in fast. The sky wasn't completely black, but the gray was deepening. He expected it to freeze again tonight. Spring hadn't been here after all. He felt more alone than he ever had in his life.

Chapter Fifteen

The next morning Katrina lay in the bed and watched the new day arrive. She was tired in her bones, but she hadn't been able to sleep. It hadn't taken the sheriff's department more than a half hour to talk to the two men they'd arrested and completely search Leanne's car. They'd found two big black bags stuffed with marijuana in the trunk. Apparently, Walker had been part of a group selling drugs and had tried to steal from the others. Leanne said he must have thought her car would be a better hiding place than his pickup truck.

Katrina wasn't so sure she'd ever forgive Walker for putting her sister in that kind of danger.

When the sheriff and his colleagues had

left, Katrina went to her room upstairs and shut the door. She missed supper, but she'd managed to cry all her tears. Charley and Edith had come to her door to try and comfort her. They confessed something to her about a prayer request Charley had made to the church and the picture Conrad had seen on her calendar. The older man seemed upset so she assured him it was all right. The emptiness she felt inside was her own making.

Edith just kept holding Katrina's hands as if there was some strength she could give to her. They prayed with her before they left and that did bring her some comfort.

It was odd, she thought to herself, as she lay there looking at the ceiling. It had taken a new broken heart for her to come home to God even though it was her first broken heart that had driven the wedge between them in the first place. Maybe things were never meant to be perfect in her life. Hard things just happened. She was learning how to live her emotions, though. Now, when she was in pain, she didn't try to hide it or to blame God for it. She was suffering through it with as much grace as she could find at the moment.

She heard the sound of a pickup truck go by in the darkness and she glanced over at the clock beside her bed. It wasn't even six o'clock yet. She was curious about the truck, but she didn't want to get up and disturb the household so she just lay in bed. Nothing much in Dry Creek was her business now anyway. She'd be leaving today.

She would go with Leanne and the boys. The lawmen were satisfied that they knew who and what had caused the upheaval at Leanne's home and she wanted to get back and put everything in place. As she told Katrina, she had a lot of thinking and praying to do before she knew what to do next.

Katrina felt the same way. She'd spend a few days helping Leanne clean up and then she'd go back to Los Angeles. In a few months, it would be as if she'd never come to this little town of Dry Creek.

Katrina blinked back her tears. Maybe she wasn't as finished crying as she had thought. She noticed that the sky had lightened considerably. She looked over at the clock and saw an hour had gone by. She might as well get up now; Edith would be starting breakfast soon and the least she could do was help.

Edith had laundered Katrina's clothes

last night so they were fresh. Her pullover smelled like some herbal something as she pulled it on over her head. Her jeans slid on easily enough. She looked at her scuffed and muddy high heels. Her tennis shoes were still in the trunk of her car but she wasn't going to put them on now. She would go out of this town in the same shoes she'd worn to enter it.

Someone started pounding outside and Edith knocked on her door at the same time. The older woman's eyes were sparkling as she asked Katrina to come downstairs with her.

"I'm glad I can help you with one last breakfast," Katrina said as she followed the older woman down the stairs. "I'm hoping to pick up some tips for those waffles you make."

"I don't think we'll have waffles this morning," Edith said.

"Well, whatever you make will be delicious."

Edith stopped at the end of the stairs and gestured to the front door. "I think you have a breakfast invitation elsewhere."

Katrina looked at her friend. "What do you mean?"

"You'll see."

Katrina walked to the front door and opened it. The outside air was cool, but that's not what she noticed first. There was a garden gnome with a bright red hat stuck in the ground at the bottom of the front steps. And he had a white piece of paper stuck to that hat with a tack.

"What?" Katrina asked again as her eyes lifted. There was a garden gnome with a yellow hat near the gate to the yard, too. And one with a blue hat in the ground down the road a little way.

"Go on, dear," Edith said as she handed Katrina her jacket.

Katrina stepped down to the first gnome and ripped off the piece of paper. She unfolded it and read, "Conrad."

She paused. She'd been angry with him for not loving her like she wanted him to. But, if she'd learned anything of late, it was that anger didn't make any relationship better. She'd like to make peace with the man before she left. Maybe then, when she remembered him, she would feel better inside.

She walked to the next gnome and his piece of paper said, "Nelson."

What was this, she wondered.

She walked along the gnome trail and picked up the third letter. "Loves."

She looked back at the house she'd just left and saw Edith standing in the doorway in her housedress and slippers, motioning for her to continue. So Katrina pressed onward. The asphalt was dry and her heels held steady. Which was more than she could say for her heart.

She pulled the fourth piece of paper from the next gnome's hand and read, "Katrina."

She started to smile then. She looked up and saw Conrad standing in the doorway of his house. The fifth gnome was by his front gate. She didn't even bother to pull the paper from his hand.

"Your whole yard is filled with gnomes," she said as she walked up to his steps.

She wanted to see Conrad's eyes. If she could only see his eyes, she would know what he meant.

"I love you." His eyes were steady.

"You're sure?"

He grinned. "Sure enough to drive to Miles City and get Earl Beck up from his bed so he'd sell me these gnomes. I had to pay double."

"It's the sweetest thing," she said. "I

know it's just for the moment, but it means a lot to know you went to the trouble."

Conrad looked at her. "It's not only for the moment. You didn't read the last note. The one where I asked you to marry me."

"You what?" she gasped.

"You know. Man and woman. Together forever."

"But I'm—" she sputtered. "I can't guarantee how long I'll live."

"Who can?" Conrad said with a nonchalance she knew had to be forced.

She didn't know what to say. She couldn't think straight. And, she felt a tear forming in one of her eyes. And then another.

"I—" she said until her throat started to close up.

Conrad reached over to a sawhorse standing on his porch and lifted up a box of tissues. He held them out to her.

Katrina took one and dabbed at her eyes. "How did you know I'd start to cry?"

"I didn't," Conrad said. "The tissues were for me in case I started to cry."

She laughed at that.

"You haven't answered," Conrad said after a moment. His voice was strained. "I know it took me too long to think things through. But that doesn't mean I don't love you. I just needed—"

"I know," Katrina said as she reached over and took his hand. "And it's okay. We can wait until I find out more from the doctors before you say any more."

"No, that's not what I'm saying at all," Conrad said. "I'm asking you to marry me as soon as you feel you can. Today. Tomorrow. Next week. I don't want to waste any more time."

She looked at his face. "But what if I—"

"Then every minute we have together needs to count," he said.

Suddenly, she wasn't alone anymore. Conrad's arms were around her and she was leaning in to him. He was willing to face his fears to love her.

"Please say yes," he whispered in her hair. "You're the only woman for me. I'll take whatever time I can get."

"In that case, yes," she said as she pulled back so she could see his eyes.

And then he kissed her. It took a second or two for her to realize that her toes were curling in her high heels. Not that it mattered when she had Conrad's arms around her to hold her up. She was where she wanted to be.

Epilogue

October that same year

Katrina came to realize that love really was timeless. A week? A month? A lifetime? Love could burn bright in any amount of time given to it. Fortunately for her, though, she could look forward to many years with Conrad.

They'd been married in late June, well over a month before she had her meeting with the oncologist. She'd carried the rose bouquet Edith kept for brides and they had cake and ice cream for the wedding reception later at the Nelson home. Katrina's two nephews had carried the rings down the aisle and Leanne had stood up with her. Uncle Charley had been Conrad's best man.

Katrina had hesitated to ask her sister to be an attendant at her wedding, but Leanne had thrown herself into the role with enthusiasm. She had separated from Walker, but she claimed that she hadn't given up on love. She was waiting, she said, for wisdom from above on what to do about Walker when he got out of jail. He had testified against the other drug dealers and they'd all been convicted.

Katrina understood Leanne's feelings. She'd support her sister in whatever she did. If her marriage could be salvaged, it would be best for all.

Katrina was coming to understand what a lifetime commitment meant. Conrad had insisted they give themselves time for a honeymoon in Glacier Park before they drove down to Los Angeles to meet with her doctor. The news on her tests couldn't have been better and, while they were there, they packed up her belongings and had them shipped back to Dry Creek.

And now she was sitting there on the porch of their newly remodeled house waiting for her husband to come home so she could show him her surprise. He'd fretted when they first married, saying he didn't want her to give up her dreams. She hadn't and he'd built a small darkroom off the kitchen for her to use.

Just then, as she glanced down the street, she saw the lights go out in the gas station. The day was growing dark. Conrad was locking up. This was her favorite time each day. She'd sit on the porch and wait for him to walk home to her, all the while looking out at their family of garden gnomes. She'd often say a prayer of thanks for having so much.

She waved at Conrad when he got as far as the asphalt street. She noticed he started to walk a little faster when he saw her. She hoped it would always be that way between them, especially now that he'd learned to waltz a little just to please her.

"Welcome home," she said when he got close enough to hear.

She stood, holding the package behind her back so the postmark wouldn't give it away.

He bounded up the steps and leaned in to kiss her. "I love it when you come out and wait for me."

"I like to visit with the gnomes."

Conrad laughed. "I know."

"I have a surprise," she said when he finished. She pulled the envelope out from behind her. "I should wait until after dinner to show it to you, but I'm so excited."

"Well, let me see then," he said as he watched her. "Is this going to be one of those happy crying moments?"

"Maybe," she said with a soft laugh and he pulled a handkerchief out of his pocket.

She slid a calendar out of the envelope.

"Romance Across America." Conrad read the title aloud and started to grin. "Don't tell me one of those photos you took ended up in that?"

Katrina opened the calendar in triumph. March was a photo of Mr. Compton and his Ella. He was holding the photo of her with such reverence, nothing but the look on his face was needed to make an unforgettable photograph. Then June was a photo of young Lucy and her boyfriend, Ben. Sweetness and love characterized that picture. The last photo she'd sent in ended up on the month of October. It was Sheriff Wall and his wife Barbara.

"Three of them," Conrad exclaimed. "They used three of your pictures!"

She nodded. When she'd asked everyone if they would mind if she sent the pictures, she'd told them she couldn't guarantee anything. They'd all happily signed their agreements, though.

"That's great," Conrad said as he picked her up and swung her around.

"And that's not even the best," she added shyly. "They said if I got enough photos they would do a coffee table book with Romance in Dry Creek pictures. People like small towns."

"My wife, the photographer," Conrad said with a proud smile. "You're putting us on the map. We don't even need that heart sign now to get tourists."

"Oh, we need the sign." She planned to give some of the money she made from the book to putting a marker up near the sign explaining how it came to be.

She knew Conrad was going to kiss her so she stretched to meet his lips halfway. From now on, that stop sign wouldn't be the only marker of true love in Dry Creek. All anyone would have to do would be to look at her face to know that love was all around in this small town.

* * * * *

Dear Reader,

I'm glad you decided to visit Dry Creek again. No one has put up a public prayer request for a wife or husband in this small town until now and I knew you'd want to see what happens. Even in a place like Dry Creek there can be too many matchmakers.

I guess our only excuse for trying to match everyone up is that we are meant to live in community. Whether married or single, child or adult, we need people to care about us. Many of us find those people in our local church. If you don't belong to a church, I'd suggest you visit one and see what happens.

Again, thanks for tuning in to the adventures in Dry Creek. If you have time, send me an e-mail through my Web site at www.janettronstad.com. Or write me in care of the editors at Steeple Hill, 233 Broadway, Suite 1001, New York, NY 10279.

Until we meet again, may God bless you.

Sincerely yours,

Janet Tronstad

QUESTIONS FOR DISCUSSION

1. In this book, Conrad Nelson has just moved to Dry Creek to be close to his only family, his uncle, Charley, and his aunt, Edith. Part of living in Dry Creek means people are going to know his business, though. How did Conrad feel when his uncle put a prayer request in the church bulletin asking God to give him a wife? Have you ever been in a situation where well-meaning people seemed to get in your business too much? The Bible calls us to be in community, does it call us to be this close, though?

2. Do you think a church should pray about people's romances? How about their finances? Their political decisions? Their ethics? Where is the dividing line between concern and nosiness?

3. Conrad had a hard life. Why is he reluctant to risk loving someone? Have you had a bad experience that has made you hesitate to get close to people? How could people in the

church have made this situation better? And what would have made it worse?

4. Katrina Britton had a difficult past, too. Why did she feel God betrayed her? Have you ever felt God has betrayed your trust? What difference has this made in your life?

5. What prompted Katrina to quit her secretarial job and pursue her dream of being a professional photographer? Have you ever had a dream like that? What did you do—or what will you do—to make it come true?

6. Katrina learned to see things differently when she gave up trying to control them. Why do you think she found it so hard to give up control?

7. Conrad was afraid to love someone too much, because he didn't want them to die. This is understandable. How do we get courage to love anyone? What would you have told Conrad if you could have talked with him?

8. Aunt Edith opens her home to four people she barely knows: Katrina, her sister and her nephews. The Bible tells us to be hospitable. Would you do the same thing? Why or why not?

9. Conrad doesn't realize he loves Katrina until it's almost too late. Have you ever realized the importance of someone only when it's time to say goodbye (i.e., realizing all your parents have done for you as it's time to move on to college, coming to appreciate a friend when it's time for them to leave)?

10. Katrina's sister has to decide whether or not to divorce her husband, Walker. What do you think she will do?

Here's a sneak preview of
THE RANCHER'S PROMISE
by Jillian Hart
Available in June 2010
from Love Inspired

"So, are you back to stay?" Justin's deep voice hid any shades of emotion. Was he fishing for information or was he finally about to say "I told you so"?

"I'll probably go back to teaching in Dallas, but things could change. I'll just have to wait and see." The things in life she used to think were so important no longer mattered. Standing on her own two feet, building a life for herself, healing her wounds—that did.

"And this man you married?" he asked. "Did he leave you or did you leave him?"

"He threw me out." She waited for Justin's reaction. Surely a man with that severe a frown on his face was about to take delight in the irony. She'd turned down Justin's love, and her husband of five years had thrown away hers. If she were Justin, she would want her off his land.

"You were nothing but honest with me back then." He leaned against the railing, the wind raking his dark hair, and a different emotion passed across his hard countenance. "I was the one who never listened. I loved you so much, I don't think I could hear anything but what I wanted."

"I loved you, too. I wish I could have been different for you." Helpless, she took another step toward the driveway. She didn't know how to thank him. He could be treating her a lot worse right now, and she would deserve it. "Goodbye, Justin."

"I suppose you need a job?"

"I'll figure out something." Need a job? No, she was frantic for one. How did she tell him the truth?

Find out in THE RANCHER'S PROMISE
Available June 2010 from Love Inspired

Love Inspired™
HISTORICAL
INSPIRATIONAL HISTORICAL ROMANCE

Engaging stories of romance,
adventure and faith,
these novels are set in
various historical periods
from biblical times
to World War II.

NOW AVAILABLE!

Steeple
Hill®

For exciting stories that reflect traditional values,
visit:
www.SteepleHill.com

LIHDIR08